DERRICK

DERRICK

TEXAS BOUDREAU BROTHERHOOD

By

KATHY IVAN

COPYRIGHT

Derrick – Original Copyright © July 2021 by Kathy Ivan

Cover by Elizabeth Mackay

Release date: July 2021
Print Edition

All Rights Reserved

DERRICK – Texas Boudreau Brotherhood Book #9

"In Shiloh Springs, Kathy Ivan has crafted warm, engaging characters that will steal your heart and a mystery that will keep you reading to the very last page." Barb Han, USA TODAY and Publisher's Weekly Bestselling Author

Kathy Ivan's books are addictive, you can't read just one." Susan Stoker, NYT Bestselling Author

BOOKS BY KATHY IVAN

www.kathyivan.com/books.html

TEXAS BOUDREAU BROTHERHOOD

Rafe

Antonio

Brody

Ridge

Lucas

Heath

Shiloh

Chance

Derrick

Dane (coming soon)

NEW ORLEANS CONNECTION SERIES

Desperate Choices

Connor's Gamble

Relentless Pursuit

Ultimate Betrayal

Keeping Secrets

Sex, Lies and Apple Pies

Deadly Justice

Wicked Obsession

Hidden Agenda

Spies Like Us

Fatal Intentions

New Orleans Connection Series Box Set: Books 1-3

New Orleans Connection Series Box Set: Books 4-7

Hello Readers,

Welcome to Shiloh Springs, Texas! Don't you just love a small Texas town where the people are neighborly, the gossip plentiful, and the heroes are…well, heroic, not to mention easy on the eyes! I love everything about Texas, which I why I've made the great state my home for over thirty years. There's no other place like it. From the delicious Tex-Mex food and downhome barbecue, the majestic scenery and friendly atmosphere, the people and places of the Lone Star state are as unique and colorful as you'll find anywhere.

The Texas Boudreau Brotherhood series centers on a group of foster brothers, men who would have ended up in the system if not for Douglas and Patricia Boudreau. Instead of being hardened by life's hardships and bad circumstances beyond their control, they found a family who loved and accepted them, and gave them a place to call home. Sometimes brotherhood is more than sharing the same DNA.

While there are a lot of Boudreau brothers (and we can't forget Nica), there are also some interesting characters that have made their way into Shiloh Springs and into readers hearts, and I know you're curious about some of them. So, I'm going to be writing stories about some of them, like Antonio's boss with the FBI, Derrick Williamson. He's been back and forth between Austin and Shiloh Springs enough that the locals have gotten to know him well. Now, it's your turn to find out more about Derrick.

Derrick isn't a Boudreau per se, but he's been around the Boudreau family long enough that I thought he needed his own story. Derrick's got his hands full when his ex-wife drops his 9-year-old son in his lap and leaves for parts unknown. Wanting to give his son a stable life, Derrick decides to buy a second home in Shiloh Springs. The added perk is he'll get to see a lot more of Daisy Parker, the owner of the local diner. I hope I did Derrick, Ian, and Daisy's story justice in the telling.

If you've read my other romantic suspense books (the New Orleans Connection series and Cajun Connection series), you'll be familiar with the Boudreau name. Turns out there are a whole lot of Boudreaus out there, just itching to have their stories told. (Douglas is the brother of Gator Boudreau, patriarch of the New Orleans branch of the Boudreau family. Oh, and did I mention they have another brother – Hank "The Tank" Boudreau?)

So, sit back and relax. The pace of small-living might be less hectic than the big city, but small towns hold secrets, excitement, and heroes who ride to the rescue. And don't you just love a Texas cowboy?

Kathy Ivan

EDITORIAL REVIEWS

"In Shiloh Springs, Kathy Ivan has crafted warm, engaging characters that will steal your heart and a mystery that will keep you reading to the very last page."

—Barb Han, *USA TODAY* and Publisher's Weekly Bestselling Author

"Kathy Ivan's books are addictive, you can't read just one."

—Susan Stoker, NYT Bestselling Author

"Kathy Ivan's books give you everything you're looking for and so much more."

—Geri Foster, USA Today and NYT Bestselling Author of the Falcon Securities Series

"This is the first I have read from Kathy Ivan and it won't be the last."

—Night Owl Reviews

"I highly recommend Desperate Choices. Readers can't go wrong here!"

—Melissa, Joyfully Reviewed

"I loved how the author wove a very intricate storyline with plenty of intriguing details that led to the final reveal…"

—Night Owl Reviews

Desperate Choices—Winner 2012 International Digital Award—Suspense

Desperate Choices—Best of Romance 2011 –Joyfully Reviewed

DEDICATIONS AND ACKNOWLEDGEMENTS

To my readers—those who've been with me since the beginning, and those who've just joined me on my journey, you are the reason I keep writing.

To my sister, Mary. She knows why.

As always, I dedicate this and every book to my mother, Betty Sullivan. Her love of reading introduced me to books at a young age. I will always cherish the memories of talking books and romance with her. I know she's looking down on me and smiling.

More about Kathy and her books can be found at

WEBSITE:
www.kathyivan.com

Follow Kathy on Facebook at
facebook.com/kathyivanauthor

Follow Kathy on Twitter at
twitter.com/@kathyivan

Follow Kathy at BookBub
bookbub.com/profile/kathy-ivan

NEWSLETTER SIGN UP

Don't want to miss out on any new books, contests, and free stuff? Sign up to get my newsletter. I promise not to spam you, and only send out notifications/e-mails whenever there's a new release or contest/giveaway. Follow the link and join today!

http://eepurl.com/baqdRX

DERRICK

CHAPTER ONE

"Anything interesting happening today, Daisy gal?"

Leaning her hip against the counter in the diner's kitchen, Daisy Parker watched Ike scramble eggs on the flattop with the expertise of a five-star gourmet chef. She could almost forget he was a short-order cook, because the man had a palate of a food critic and the skills of a French-trained gourmand.

He added salt and pepper and a heaping handful of sharp cheddar, and within moments piled it onto a plate with bacon and sausage. Two slices of buttered Texas Toast were added to the order, along with a single orange slice. She remembered him teasing her in the past, calling it fancying up the plate.

"I've got the rest of the afternoon off, and all day tomorrow. Jackie is going to cover my shift, while I spend a few hours pampering myself from head to toe."

Ike placed the hot plate on the counter and grinned at her. "Guess that means Derrick Williamson's coming to town."

Heat flooded her face, and she knew the blush would be

visible with her fair skin. Being a natural blonde, she tended to blush easily and turned a most unbecoming shade of bright red. She'd always wished she were one of those women who look adorable when they blushed—she looked like she had a two-day-old sunburn. She fingered a lock of her hair, loving the dark blue streaks she'd applied a couple days earlier. If there was one vice she'd claim proudly, it was experimenting with her hair color. Blues, greens, pinks – she'd worn a virtual rainbow of hues over the past couple of years. Called it her signature, her style. All she cared was it made her feel young and alive, and if some of the fuddy-duddies didn't like it, though.

"I have no idea if Derrick's coming to town. Not like it's my business."

Ike slid a stack of flapjacks with link sausages beside the scrambled egg plate and added the bottle of maple syrup to the tray. Not the cheap stuff, either. There were only a couple of things Ike insisted on when he was cooking. Fresh ingredients whenever possible, and real honest-to-goodness maple syrup. Since he was one of the best cooks west of the Mississippi, she indulged his whims. It was a small price to pay to keep the old grump happy. But he was her old grump, and she adored him.

"Seems like Williamson's been showing up more and more lately. How do you feel about that, Daisy gal?"

"He's had lots of work in the area recently. It's not like he's coming just to see me, Ike."

"Seriously? Are you blind? Haven't you noticed how he hangs around the diner when he's in town? And don't tell me Patti Boudreau wouldn't feed him up at the Big House, the way she does all the strays who end up in Shiloh Springs. He ain't hanging around the diner to see my ugly mug." He paused and scratched at the perpetual salt-and-pepper stubble that seemed ever present on his chin. "Of course, could be he keeps coming back for the food."

"I'm sure that's it." She grinned at Ike, then picked up the two plates and added them to the tray. With an almost imperceptible grunt, she hefted it high and carried the loaded tray through the swinging door separating the kitchen from the dining room. A fleeting thought raced through her mind. Could Ike be right? Derrick did tend to hang around the diner a lot when he was in Shiloh Springs, but she figured he liked the food, and it was a central location for meeting with everyone, especially Rafe and Antonio.

Stopping beside a booth toward the back of the diner, she smiled at Jill Monroe and Lucas Boudreau. They were cuddled together on one side of the booth, his arm around Jill's shoulders. Daisy was thrilled for them both because she knew and respected them. Lucas had loved Jill for the longest time, and more than once he'd confided in Daisy how he felt about the town's pretty baker. How he'd lost her through his stupidity and couldn't figure out how to win her back. Luckily, he'd gotten his head screwed on straight, and now they were getting their happily ever after.

A tiny surge of the green-eyed monster rearing its ugly head made her wonder if she'd ever get her own Mr. Wonderful. She quashed it down, refusing to let the what ifs and maybes take away from being happy for her friends. Too bad all those Boudreau men were like brothers to her, because any one of them would make an ideal mate. Oh, well...

"Here you go, folks. Ike said to eat it while it's hot."

"It looks delicious. Tell him thanks." Lucas dug into the pancakes like he hadn't seen real food in days. Daisy grinned. Now there was a sight she never got tired of: Watching people dig into their orders and finding real enjoyment from the meal. It gave her a sense of rightness, and she never regretted moving to Shiloh Springs to help her uncle with the diner after his stroke.

"Daisy, want to get together later? We need to go over what you're going to need for next week." Jill's sweet smile matched her personality. Several months ago, she had entered a business arrangement with Ms. Patti and opened a bakery on Main Street. Almost from the start, she'd made a business agreement with Jill to supply baked goods for the diner. Ike might be an amazing cook, but a baker? Only if you wanted to eat burnt cookies, half-baked pies, and sawdust cakes. Jill's bakery, *How Sweet It Is*, had become a lifesaver to patrons of the diner who wanted something sweet after their meal.

"Can't today, Jill. I've got plans this afternoon. How

about we get together on Monday?"

"That works. I'll text you with a time if that's okay?"

"Sounds good. Y'all need anything else?"

Lucas shook his head, a forkful of pancakes halfway to his mouth. When Daisy's gaze met Jill's, they both laughed, knowing he didn't have a clue. Most of their business meetings consisted of setting a schedule of baked treats for the diner, and then drinking coffee and sampling new flavors or products Jill came up with. The winners were sold in the bakery. The losers went into their bellies. As far as Daisy was concerned, it was a win-win.

"So," Jill's voice held the slightest hint of laughter, "you've got plans this afternoon. Does that mean Derrick's coming to town?"

Daisy threw her hands up in the air. "Why is everybody assuming because I'm taking a day off it has anything to do with Derrick Williamson? Honestly, I don't have a clue what the man's plans are, or whether he's headed for Shiloh Springs. I have an appointment for a total spa day. Manicure, pedicure, facial, and massage. It's been way too long since I took a 'me' day."

"What a great idea. You deserve to pamper yourself. You work yourself ragged, making sure the diner is running smoothly. If I'd known earlier, we could have made a day of it. Next time, call me. I'll gather the other ladies, and we'll have a total women's only party." Jill shot Lucas a side-eyed glare. "It's not like the guys don't get together all the time and have their guy's night out. We should totally do the same."

"You're on." Daisy gave Jill a high five and left them to their food. She'd spotted Jackie a couple minutes ago and wanted to go over things with her before she headed out. Jackie was new to Shiloh Springs, having moved to town six weeks earlier. When she'd applied for the part-time waitress position, Daisy took one look at her resume and hired her on the spot. She hadn't regretted the decision. Jackie hadn't missed a shift and worked harder than any waitress she'd had before.

"Hey, boss lady. Anything I need to worry about?"

"Nope. The breakfast crowd was insane. The lunch rush is pretty much over, so you shouldn't have any problems. Ike's got your back if you run into anything you're not sure about. I'm only a phone call away if there's an emergency."

Jackie tied a pristine white apron around her waist, covering the light-colored jeans and red T-shirt, the standard uniform for wait staff at the diner. Daisy wasn't too concerned about having fancy uniforms; comfort over frills was her motto. Besides, it wasn't the clothes that kept the patrons coming back. It was the friendly atmosphere and Ike's famous five-alarm chili. And his chicken-fried steak. And his pot roast. Of course, everybody knew the biggest draw was his burgers. People had been known to drive fifty miles or more just to get one of Ike's burgers. The man had the magic touch when it came to the classic diner staples.

She'd begged and pleaded to know what he did to make them taste so good, but he simply grinned, said it was a secret family recipe, and he was taking it to the grave.

"Go. Have fun, you deserve it." Jackie stuffed a ticket book in the front pocket of the apron, ready to take over for the afternoon. She'd also handle opening the diner tomorrow morning. A tiny itch at the back of her brain protested the thought of somebody else taking care of her baby, her pride and joy, but she pushed the unwarranted thought down. Jackie hadn't done a thing to make her feel that way, and Ike would be here, so nothing bad was going to happen.

Daisy walked the few steps toward the kitchen and pushed open the swinging door and waved at Ike. "I'm out of here. Jackie's got the front covered. Call me if the place catches fire."

"Get out of here, Daisy gal. The place will still be standing when you come back."

Shaking her head, she grinned and turned to leave, but froze in her tracks. Illuminated in the open doorway of the diner stood the man who'd been occupying more and more of her thoughts over the last few months. Dressed in a pair of dark jeans and a white button-front shirt, a tan cowboy hat atop his head, he looked like he'd just rode into town after a day working the ranch. Nobody looking at him dressed this casually would mistake him for the man in charge of the Austin branch of the FBI. He reached up and removed the cowboy hat, revealing close-cropped sandy brown hair with golden highlights from the sunshine behind him. She'd always secretly wished he'd grow it a little longer. Her fingers itched to slide through it because it looked soft and silky and oh-so-touchable. When his brown-eyed gaze met hers, a slow, sexy smile curved his lips upward. A faint fluttering in the pit of her stomach had her clenching her hands at her sides. Dang, the man was fine, fine, fine.

Movement at his side drew her eyes to the mini-me version standing at his side, shifting restlessly from foot to foot. She'd met Derrick's son a couple times when he'd brought the nine-year-old into the diner when they'd been in Shiloh Springs. Ian Williamson was a cute kid, looking like a youthful version of his father. Right now, though, he didn't look all that happy to be here. His ever-present video game was clutched in his hand. When his father leaned closer and whispered something, Daisy couldn't help seeing the kid's eye roll. Oh, yeah, somebody didn't want to be here. Was it the diner that drew his displeasure, or the fact he was in small-town Texas instead of his condo in the big city?

"Good afternoon, Derrick. Ian. Nice to see you." Daisy couldn't help noticing the way Derrick gave her a once over, then reached out and tugged on one of the deep blue streaks in her hair.

"Hello, Daisy. I like the blue."

"Thanks. Feel free to grab a seat wherever you'd like. Jackie will be with you in a minute to take your order." She hitched the strap of her purse higher on her shoulder, ready to shimmy past the taller man. Broad shoulders took up almost the entire opening, and her breath caught in the back of her throat at the thought of her body sliding past his. She swallowed and almost reached up to check for drool.

"Ian?" Derrick's voice was low and filled with an unspoken command. The look he shot his son brooked no defiance. There was no anger there, simply a questioning look that accompanied his one word.

"Sorry, Dad, I forgot." Ian scuffed one tennis shoe against the linoleum floor, not meeting her eyes. "Hi, Daisy. It's nice to see you."

Her brows rose at the obviously rehearsed greeting. Shoulders shaking with suppressed laughter, she answered. "Hi, Ian. It's nice to see you, too."

"Go ahead and grab us a booth, kiddo. I need to talk to Daisy for a second. Order me a burger and fries if Jackie gets there before me."

Without a word, Ian raced toward the back, grabbing the last booth and clamoring onto the seat. Immediately the video game was held in both hands, his concentration lost to everything but the battle taking place in front of his face. Daisy wondered if she'd ever been that focused and driven over something so innocent and frivolous as a game.

"How've you been, Daisy?" Derrick's deep voice pulled her back to where she stood, and the quivering inside her intensified.

"Fine. What brings you to Shiloh Springs this time—

business or pleasure?"

"Mostly pleasure. I have a quick meeting with Rafe and then I've got the whole weekend to relax. And by relax, I mean Ms. Patti is going to show me a couple of places to rent. It doesn't make sense to keep staying at the Creekside Inn, since we've been coming here so much. There are things about Shiloh Springs I like—quite a lot." His words were accompanied by a quick grin.

"That's wonderful. I'm sure she'll find you a great place. Are you looking at apartments or houses?"

"Probably a mix of both. I want someplace where Ian will feel at home. He's been through so much upheaval in the last year, I want to give him a sense of stability. Let him know that I'm not going anywhere, and he's got a father he can count on."

Though they'd talked multiple times whenever he'd been in the diner, and even once when they'd met up at Gracie's Grounds, there was so much she didn't know about the man. They'd tried a couple of times to have dinner, but life seemed determined to conspire against them. He'd gotten called back to Austin twice, having to cancel. Another time the circuit box at the diner got fried and hadn't that been a fun and expensive night? She'd pretty much decided Fate didn't mean for them to be anything but friends. So why did the man fascinate her more than any other? All the Boudreaus liked and respected him and considered him a friend. That counted for a lot in her books, but as far as romance and Derrick Williamson—it wasn't gonna happen.

"I don't know all the details, but I'm sure you're a good father. Give him time. Change is never easy, especially for a kid."

"Most kids don't have their mothers abandon them."

His words hit her like a slap to the face. While she'd known he was divorced and had been for several years, she had no idea Ian's mother had walked out, leaving her child behind. She couldn't imagine not wanting your own flesh and blood. A flood of memories washed through her, and she wanted to run. As fast and as far as her feet would carry her, away from the anguish, hurt, and disappointment. Instead, she pasted a smile on her face, not wanting Derrick to see how his words affected her.

"I'm sorry. I had no idea." Reaching forward, she laid her hand on his forearm, feeling the tightly bunched muscles beneath her fingertips. "Anything I can do to help?"

"Thanks, I might take you up on that sometime. Right now, all I can do is let him know he's wanted and that I'll never leave him. Never." Daisy heard the ring of promise in his words, knew he meant them with every breath.

"Well, then, I'll let y'all get your lunch. I've got plans for a total head-to-toe makeover."

His hand reached up and tugged lightly on the dark blue streak again. "Leave the blue. It suits you."

"Alright. I kind of like it too. See you guys later."

"Bye, Daisy."

Taking a deep breath, she walked out the front door and climbed behind the wheel of her little yellow Bug. She loved the vivid, bright color, and didn't care that it was older than dirt. It had belonged to her uncle, and he'd driven in for years before his stroke. When she'd moved back to Shiloh Springs to help take care of him, he'd paid Frank at the garage to make sure it was mechanically sound and had it painted the brilliant and bold color. He'd gifted it to her, along with the diner. While he'd recovered mentally from the stroke, and was sharp as a tack, physically he'd never be the same. The unexpected cardiovascular attack had damaged his heart as well as paralyzed his entire right side. He had trouble breathing, walking was out of the question, and he'd become dependent on a wheelchair and an electric scooter when he wanted mobility.

Pulling away from the diner, she headed for the day spa, more than ready to get a little pampering and to forget about everything but enjoying a little TLC.

Too bad she couldn't stop thinking about a tall, dark Texan who could never be hers.

CHAPTER TWO

"Did Jackie take your order?"

His son shrugged his shoulders, eyes glued to his video game. Derrick fought the urge to lean forward and bang his head against the Formica tabletop. Ian had barely uttered a word the entire drive from Austin. Shiloh Springs wasn't his favorite spot; Derrick got it. Maneuvering the rapidly changing mindset of a nine-year-old reminded him of tiptoeing through a minefield. The past few months served to emphasize the vast divide between him and his son, and his mother's decision to sign away all rights to her only child and head out for parts unknown hadn't helped.

"Ian."

Silence was the only answer he got.

"Ian." This time his voice brooked no disobedience.

"Yeah?"

"Are you ever going to talk to me?"

"About what?" The petulant expression on his son's face made it clear to Derrick Ian knew exactly what he wanted to discuss.

"Your mother, your move to Austin, living with me.

Take your pick."

"Dad, it is what it is. It's no big deal."

"It is a big deal. I'm sorry things have been crazy since your mother left, but she was unhappy."

"She wasn't the only one." Ian's words were whispered so soft Derrick wondered if he'd actually heard them.

When Jackie stopped beside their booth with their order, he smiled, noting his son's lunch order. A huge bowl of chicken and dumplings and a couple of pieces of cornbread. Comfort food at its finest, and Daisy's Diner made some of the best he'd ever tasted, outside his grandmother's. His own plate held a bacon cheeseburger and a mound of fries, hot, crispy, and golden. His mouth watered when the scent of grilled meat hit his system. The only thing that would make this better was Daisy sticking around.

Since it didn't look like Ian wanted to talk about his issues, Derrick decided a change of topic might work.

"Ms. Patti is taking us house shopping this afternoon. Anything special you want in our weekend home?"

Ian looked up, a spoonful of food halfway to his mouth. "You're asking me?"

"Sure. You'll be living there too, so you get some say in what you want."

He watched his son digest his words, a contemplative expression crossing his face. Mentally crossing his fingers, he hoped his son didn't come up with some outlandish request like a moat filled with crocodiles or a pit filled with rattlesnakes. He wouldn't put it past him, because living with a nine-year-old had proved they had vivid imaginations and could come up with the craziest ideas from one breath to the next.

"Can I have my own bedroom?"

"Of course. You'll be getting your own bathroom too, which you'll have to keep clean because I'm tired of your stinky underwear and socks all over mine. Plus, leaving all that toothpaste in the sink after you spit it out? Son, you don't live in a barn."

"Oh, that would be cool."

Derrick shook his head, the corners of his lips tugging up. "We are not living in a barn."

"But, I saw this thing on TV the other night…"

"No barn. We can look at apartments, maybe a condo, or a house. And no underground bunkers either."

Ian laughed and the sound was like music to Derrick. There hadn't been nearly as much laughter from the past few months, and he hated that his son was unhappy. He was too young to have his life upended, turned upside down.

"If we got a house, it would have a yard, right?"

"We could talk to Ms. Patti, make sure we looked at ones that have a yard."

"What about a pool?"

Derrick drew in a deep breath. He knew Ian hadn't been around water a lot growing up. His ex had an obsessive fear of the water and never learned to swim. Ever since he'd moved into Derrick's Austin condo, he'd caught him eyeing the pool more than once, an expression of longing in his gaze, which he quickly disguised whenever he spotted Derrick watching him.

"Let's add that to the list."

After a few seconds, Ian nodded and shoved another spoonful of chicken and dumplings into his mouth. When his stomach growled, Derrick picked up his burger and took a big bite. An explosion of flavor followed each chew, and he mentally thanked Ike for such a great burger. Dipping one of his fries into the ketchup container, he popped it into his mouth, before he caught sight of Ian eyeing his fries hungrily.

He waved a hand toward his plate. "Go ahead."

"Thanks." Almost faster than his eye could follow, two fries disappeared from his plate, shoved into his son's gaping maw. The kid was a bottomless pit, and he was fairly sure he'd have to take out a loan just to keep him in tacos and sodas.

When the bell above the front door jangled, he automatically looked up and spotted Patricia Boudreau entering. The diminutive woman glanced around the diner, seeing him almost immediately. A warm smile graced her face. Having gotten to know her over the past year, Derrick knew that she was a beautiful woman inside and out. A loving, generous, kind spirit, she'd made him feel welcome in Shiloh Springs and an honorary part of their family. Their clan, as she called them.

Heading toward them like a whirlwind, he heard the gentle clackety-clack of her heels on the black-and-white tile floor. The sound triggered a sense of peace deep within, almost a sense of homecoming.

Ian leaned forward and whispered conspiratorially, "Sounds like Ms. Patti's coming."

Funny, guess his son recognized the older woman's footsteps. He wondered if Ian got the same sense of contentment in her presence. Derrick stood when she approached their booth.

"Hello, Derrick. Ian. My goodness, that looks delicious. Ike makes the best cornbread, but I haven't been able to get him to share his recipe." She winked at Ian. "I'm not giving up yet. I'll get that recipe, one way or another."

"It's really good. Would you like some, ma'am?" Ian slid the half-empty plate closer to Ms. Patti.

"That's very sweet, Ian. Thank you, but I've already eaten. I thought I'd join you, maybe take a few notes while y'all finish your meal if that's okay?"

Ian scooted over on the booth seat, and Ms. Patti slid in beside him. Derrick resumed his seat, catching the sparkle in the other woman's gaze. She had a way of making everyone around her at ease. It was a gift, Derrick knew, because most people rarely bothered, especially with kids. Most of the time, the children got ignored, especially when the grownups had business to discuss.

"I brought a list of local places we can look at, but I need some input from you both. Mind if I ask a few questions, so I can get a feel for what would suit you both?"

"Dad says we can get a pool." Ian kept chewing as he spoke, and a few cornbread crumbs flew onto the tabletop.

"Buddy, don't talk with your mouth full. Ms. Patti will wait for your answer. Besides, I don't want you to choke."

Derrick watched Ms. Patti try to hide her smile. She was used to having to remind boys about their manners, having raised eleven of them herself. How in the world she'd managed that, he hadn't a clue. He was having enough trouble dealing with one and he hadn't even hit puberty yet.

"Let's add a pool to the top of the list. I wish I'd have thought of having one when we first moved to the Big House. Sometimes, with these hot Texas summers, the best I could manage was squirting my boys with a hose. Of course, that ended when they discovered swimming in the creek was almost as much fun as having a pool."

"A creek? Isn't that dangerous?" Ian had stopped eating, his attention locked on Ms. Patti, his eyes round and eager.

"It can be if you're not careful. Douglas and I laid down the law right away when we found out they'd been swimming in the creek that runs across our property. No swimming alone, ever. It's too dangerous. No swimming if the weather is bad. Flash floods can happen within minutes, and rushing water is nothing to joke about. I've seen creek water rise and carry away a whole car. The water is stronger than you think, and you can get washed away before somebody can rescue you."

"You'll stick to pools, at least until I know you can swim." Derrick swallowed down his fear at the thought of losing Ian.

"Dad…"

Ms. Patti simply smiled and made a note on her pad. "What else are you looking for? Two bedrooms, maybe an office?"

"I think we can get by with two bedrooms. I'm not planning on bringing work with me when we're in Shiloh Springs. I'll set up a desk in my bedroom if I need that option."

He watched Ian's shoulders unclench as he relaxed on hearing his words. How bad were things, that he hadn't even realized his son was worried about his dad working on their long weekends and time off?

"What else? Tell me honestly," she looked directly at Ian, "do you want an apartment or a house? Maybe a condo?"

"That's up to my dad." Ian shrugged and shoveled a spoonful of chicken and dumplings into his mouth.

"Oh, I know what your dad wants." Ms. Patti glanced at Derrick and gave him a subtle wink. "I want to know what you want, Ian. You're going to be living there, too. You should be comfortable in your own home."

"I…I guess I'd like a house. Before, when I lived with—"

Though he broke off, Derrick knew he'd been going to

talk about living with his mother. He couldn't count the number of times he'd gotten up in the middle of the night, and found Ian huddled on the couch, the TV volume low, because he couldn't sleep. Although he hated to admit it, he knew his son still wasn't sure Derrick wasn't going to abandon him too.

"Our first choice would be houses, Ms. Patti. Something with a yard. Nothing too big, because I don't want to have to deal with lots of upkeep, but we," he gestured with his thumb between him and Ian, "can handle a lawnmower."

"Gotcha. I have a couple of rental places to show you. Move-in ready, no handyman specials. They're amenable to small changes, such as painting bedrooms and things. Next question, do you want them furnished, or will you be wanting to bring your own stuff?"

"I'm thinking we should probably do furnished. Once we're settled, we might want to get a few things of our own, but to start out…"

"I understand, and I think that's a good idea. I'm heading over to my office to print out a few listings. Y'all finish your lunch and you can meet me over there when you're finished. And don't forget to have some of the chocolate chip cake. Jill made some earlier this morning, and it's delicious."

"Thanks, Ms. Patti. We won't be long."

"Thank you, ma'am." Ian stuck out his hand, and Ms. Patti shook it. Derrick felt a warmth filling him, so proud of his little man. He was trying, he'd give him that. Now if he could just provide him with the stability he needed, he'd figure out that he was safe and secure, and he could finally relax and be a kid.

After Ms. Patti left, Derrick made quick work of his bacon cheeseburger. Glancing at Ian, he had to bite his cheek to keep from laughing. Ian was scraping the bowl, trying to get every last drop of the chicken and dumplings. Good thing they were in public, or he'd probably be licking the bowl clean.

"Are we getting the cake?"

"Why not?" Derrick waved at Jackie and ordered two pieces of the cake Ms. Patti mentioned. He was familiar with Jill's baking, having sampled more than his fair share of *How Sweet It Is* goods every time he visited Shiloh Springs. When the two huge slices of cake arrived, he inhaled deeply, wondering if he should have ordered one piece to split with his son.

Ian attacked his piece with gusto, shoveling the chocolatey gooey treat into his mouth, only pausing long enough to take a drink before getting another. He cleaned his plate in less than two minutes. Where did he put it all? Oh, to have the metabolism of a young boy, he'd be able to eat anything he wanted to.

He managed to eat half of the huge piece of cake before pushing the remainder across the table to Ian, who demolished it in under a minute.

"You ready to go?"

Ian nodded and grabbed his game and slid from the booth. "Are you gonna see Daisy later?"

Derrick halted halfway out of the booth, surprised by his son's question. "I don't know. Why?"

"Come on, Dad, I know you like her."

"I like lots of people."

"Geez, Dad. I know you *like her* like her."

Derrick hadn't realized Ian had caught onto the fact he tended to spend a lot of his time at the diner when he visited. Guess he hadn't been subtle in his interest if his nine-year-old son noticed.

"Busted. Yeah, I like Daisy. A lot. She's nice. She's funny."

"And she's pretty. I like her rainbow hair."

Walking to the door, Derrick pulled it open, and he and Ian headed toward his truck. Climbing inside the cab, he settled in and clicked on his seatbelt, and pointed toward Ian's. Once buckled in, he turned to face his son.

"Would you be upset if I asked Daisy out?"

"You mean like on a date?"

He nodded, waiting for his son's answer. With them working their way toward a semblance of a family unit, he would never do anything to upset the applecart, no matter how much he wanted to get to know the irrepressible diner owner.

"Do you think she wants to date you? I mean, you're kind of old and all you do is work."

"Old? I'll give you old," Derrick reached across the seat, and wrapped his arm around Ian's neck, and rubbed his knuckle against his scalp, with Ian squirming to get away and giggling the whole time.

"Dad!"

Turning Ian loose, he straightened behind the steering wheel. Looked like Ian wasn't opposed to him asking Daisy out.

Maybe things were looking up—not only with his son but with his new start in Shiloh Springs.

CHAPTER THREE

Daisy threw her purse onto the console table and paused, glancing in the mirror that hung above it. Her spa day had done wonders for making her feel better, and her skin glowed after the facial. Though it was an extravagance she rarely indulged in, having a day of pampering had done her soul good.

"That you, Daisy?"

"It's me, Uncle Joe. I'll be right there."

"No hurry. I thought I heard the door and wanted to make sure I wasn't hearing things."

"Just me."

She wandered into the kitchen and found her uncle seated at the table, his wheelchair pulled close. A game of solitaire was spread out in front of him. Bending, she brushed a kiss against his cheek and moved a black ten beneath a red Jack.

"Did you have a good time with all your girly stuff?"

She smiled at his mild teasing. While he might grouse and complain, especially when he became frustrated with being stuck in a wheelchair, he'd been the one to suggest she have a special day and had even paid for the whole thing.

"I've been painted, polished, scrubbed, and massaged. I feel like a new woman." Opening the refrigerator, she pulled out the chicken she'd left marinating earlier that morning. Pulling out a cast iron skillet, she put it atop the stove and started grabbing ingredients for supper.

"Heard Derrick Williamson showed up at the diner today."

She spun around to face him, her hands on her hips. "Who told you that?"

"I'll never reveal my sources." Her uncle gave her a cocky grin and her heart melted. Having good days was getting harder and harder for him, and she cherished each and every one. The stroke had made his mobility tough, though he could stand for short periods of time. Yet his mind was sharp as a tack. Every night he whipped her at Jeopardy, his store of knowledge and trivial facts putting her to shame.

"Derrick and his son were coming into the diner as I was leaving. And for your information, he's not here to see me."

"How many times has he asked you out?"

"Uncle Joe, it's not going to work. He's got his hands full with Ian, now that his mother headed for parts unknown. Thinking about starting a relationship while trying to juggle an insecure child makes any question of dating out of the question."

"Things won't always be up in the air like this. Just don't let an opportunity to find somebody to care about slip through your fingers because you deserve to be happy, little bit."

A warm, fuzzy feeling filled her at his use of the nickname he'd given her when she was a little girl. When her mother brought her for visits to Shiloh Springs, he'd always make time to spend with her. Carrying her around on his shoulders. Taking her to the diner for ice cream. He'd made her feel special, and she'd always love him for that.

"How do chicken tacos for supper sound?"

"Works for me." He picked up all the cards and reshuffled them, spreading out the solitaire pattern again.

Turning on the fire under the cast iron skillet, Daisy set about cutting up the chicken for the tacos, adding enough spices to make the dish flavorful, but not too spicy. Uncle Joe had developed an intolerance to things that were too hot, so she'd started adjusting her recipes to accommodate him. Doing the little things to make him comfortable didn't bother her. She just wished she could do more.

Grabbing the lettuce and tomatoes from the refrigerator, she made short work of chopping and shredding, then grated some sharp cheddar cheese to add as a topping.

Wiping her hands on a kitchen towel, she turned at the sound of her cell phone ringing. She spun and raced toward the hall entry, where she'd left her purse, scrabbling inside to pull the phone free.

"Hello."

"Hi, Daisy. It's Derrick."

Her heartbeat raced at the sound of his voice. "Hi, Derrick. Are you and Ian having a good time?"

"It's been an interesting afternoon. Ms. Patti's been showing us some rental places."

Rental places? Did that mean he was moving to Shiloh Springs?

"Find anything you liked?" She made an effort to keep the overarching excitement out of her voice. Maintain calm, that's the ticket, she thought.

"Couple of houses look promising. Ian's got his heart set on a pool, so we're hedging our bets. Have some more to look at tomorrow."

"I'm sure Ms. Patti will be able to find something that'll fit your needs. Carrying her phone into the kitchen, she glanced at Uncle Joe and noted the not-disguised smirk he shot her.

"Told ya," he mouthed.

"She's amazingly insightful into what a nine-year-old boy likes. Of course, she's had lots of experience dealing with kids, so I shouldn't be surprised." Derrick paused for a moment, and Daisy heard a softly whispered conversation taking place in the background. Then he came back onto the phone.

"The reason I'm calling is to see if you'd like to have lunch with us tomorrow. Ian wants to know if you like Italian food?"

"I love Italian food. And it just so happens, I have tomorrow off. Jackie and Ike are covering for me, plus Sandy is coming in to help with the Sunday rush." Daisy wanted to do a little booty shake right there in the kitchen but didn't dare, because Uncle Joe would never let her hear the end of it, crowing about him being right.

"Does that mean you'll join us?"

"I'd love to have lunch with you and Ian."

"Great. We'll pick you up at twelve-thirty, if that works for you?"

"Alright." She rattled off her address and hung up before she made a blubbering fool of herself. Lunch with Derrick and Ian. Somehow, she had a feeling he wouldn't have to cancel on her again, not with his kiddo being along.

"You look like the cat that swallowed the canary, girl. Finally getting that date with Derrick, huh?"

"Uncle Joe, it's not a date. I'm simply going to lunch with Derrick *and* his son. Casual, no strings, nothing to get all excited about."

"I only want you to be happy, Daisy. You've dedicated your life to taking over the diner and making it successful, giving up everything to come to Shiloh Springs and take care of this old goat. Don't think I don't know about everything you sacrificed to take care of me. You deserve to find somebody who'll make you the center of his whole world, and treat you like the princess you are."

"Uncle Joe, I didn't give up anything. You are my family and I love you. I love working at the diner; it makes me happy."

"You're one of the good ones, Daisy. You know that?"

"Thank you."

"Daisy?"

"Yes?"

"Chicken's burning." He pointed to the stove and cackled like a loon when she scrambled with the cast iron skillet, muttering under her breath. Grabbing plates out of the cupboard, she started assembling their dinner.

And did her best to stop wondering why Derrick asked her out.

"She said yes."

"Okay."

Ian sat curled with his legs tucked beneath him on the sofa in their room. They'd checked into the B&B earlier, before heading to the diner and their meeting with Ms. Patti. Derrick wasn't surprised Ian headed straight for the TV as soon as they'd gotten back from looking at potential houses. Now he sat, his attention fixated at some show. Glancing at the screen, he couldn't make heads or tails of what was happening. He spotted the logo of a popular kid's channel in the corner and figured it didn't look too advanced for Ian's years.

"What did you think of the places we saw? Any one in

particular you liked better than the others?"

Ian shrugged and Derrick wanted to pull his hair out. He was clueless on how to communicate with his son, and nothing he'd tried seemed to be working. Although he'd spent every minute he could with Ian after the divorce, the truth was he had no idea what his mother might have told him about their split. How do you combat something you're unsure of? Add in the fact he worked more than the normal forty-hour week with the FBI, and Ian probably felt like he'd been abandoned by both parents.

"I liked the blue one with the white shutters. Both of the bedrooms were pretty big, right?"

"I guess."

"Buddy, talk to me. What's going on inside your head? Do you hate it here, because we don't have to move."

At his son's shrug, Derrick balled up his fists, fighting the urge to let loose a primal scream. What was it going to take to get through to him? Because he'd do it.

"Look, if you want to go back to Austin, we can leave right now. I can call Daisy and tell her we have to cancel lunch tomorrow. She sounded kind of excited, but you come first. Always."

Ian's head jerked toward him, his big blue eyes wary. "Wouldn't that hurt her feelings?"

"Probably, but your feelings matter, too."

The hand holding the TV remote fiddled with the buttons, and Ian's look of concentration almost made Derrick smile.

"It wouldn't be right to ask Daisy to come to lunch and then not go. We better stay."

Derrick plopped down on the sofa beside Ian, and ruffled his hand through his son's hair, grinning when he ducked and tried to get away. Reaching across the space, he tickled Ian, hearing his delighted squeals of laughter as he wriggled in a vain attempt to get away.

"Dad! Stop!"

Derrick tickled him for another minute or so, before he eased up, sitting back and watching Ian grin. Kids' moods were so mercurial, flipping off and on a dime. He'd get used to it eventually.

"You hungry?"

Ian tilted his head to the side before answering. "I could eat."

"How about we have a great big banana split for dinner?"

"Awesome."

"Come on, kiddo. Ice cream for dinner. Just don't tell Ms. Patti tomorrow. She'll take away my good dad badge."

"My lips are sealed. Except for when I'm eating the ice cream."

"Smart kid. Let's go."

CHAPTER FOUR

Daisy barely made it home before Derrick's big pickup pulled into her driveway. She'd headed to church earlier that morning. Sometimes she felt guilty that she couldn't make services very often, but she had to keep the diner open every day, though she made it when she could.

The pickup's tires crunched against the pea gravel in front of the house. Uncle Joe converted the front yard and the drive into more drought-tolerant foliage after his stroke, knowing he wouldn't be able to tend to the yard work and lawn mowing needed to keep nature from taking over.

She waved before climbing from the front porch and headed toward the truck, noticing Ian seated in the passenger seat. Derrick climbed from the driver's side and met her when she got to the car.

"Good morning, Daisy. You look lovely this morning."

"Thanks. I went to church this morning."

"I'm looking forward to getting back into church, once we're in Shiloh Springs."

The passenger door flew open and Ian jumped out, waving at Daisy, before scrambling around to the back seat of the extended cab. His grin was infectious, making Daisy's lips curl up in response.

"Shall we?"

"Absolutely, I'm starving."

Derrick helped her into the passenger side, and jogged around the front of the truck, before climbing behind the wheel. "Ian and I found this great Italian place just over the county line in Santa Lucia. We've eaten there a couple of times, and really like it."

"I'm game. I haven't had really good Italian in a while."

"They've got good pizza," Ian added from the back seat. "We eat a lot of pizza at home, but this place is way cooler."

Daisy shot a look at Derrick, and he shrugged, giving her a halfhearted smile. "I work too much, and pizza is easy."

"How's the house hunt going? Find anything you like?"

"Ms. Patti showed us a few places yesterday. A couple of them have pools, which we both like. One had a huge backyard, but I think the house is a little too big for just the two of us."

"Give her a chance, I'm sure she'll find the perfect place for you both. She's a real estate wizard when it comes to matching up people with the right place to live." Daisy shifted in her seat, turning as much as the seatbelt allowed. "Can I ask why you're considering a place in Shiloh Springs? I thought you were some bigwig in the Austin FBI office."

Derrick chuckled, shaking his head. "I don't know about the bigwig part, but yes, my job is in Austin. Ian and I are looking for a place where we can get away for weekends and holidays, that kind of thing. Someplace away from the rat race pace of the big city where we can unwind. Since I seem to spend a lot of time in Shiloh Springs, and like the people, it seemed a good place to start looking."

Daisy swiveled in her seat to look at Ian. "Shiloh Springs is a great place. I haven't always lived here either, but I used to visit when I was about your age. My Uncle Joe owned the diner. It was named after the original Daisy Parker, who was my grandmother."

Ian watched her closely, and Daisy hoped he'd talk with her because she really wanted to get to know him. She could commiserate with him. When she'd been younger, her father walked out on her and her mother, leaving them high and dry. It forced her mother to work two jobs just to keep a roof over their heads.

"It's okay, I guess. I haven't seen a lot of kids my age."

"There are lots of kids around, trust me. Most of them have chores on Saturdays. Like your dad said, this isn't the big city. Lots of places around here have gardens where they grow vegetables. Raise chickens and rabbits and cows. If they have horses, they have to deal with all the stuff like mucking out stalls and caring for the animals. Sundays usually mean church in the morning, and then the rest of the day they're free to visit their friends and play."

"They allow animals in town?" She knew she'd captured Ian's curiosity when he asked the question. Now to keep him talking, get to know him a bit.

"Sure do. Small animals only, unless they have a farm or a ranch."

"Like the Boudreaus' ranch?"

She nodded. "Exactly like the Boudreaus' ranch. Right now, Jamie's the only kid, but from what I hear, that's about to change." At Derrick's sideways glance, she added, "Beth's pregnant."

"I want a puppy, but we can't get one. Dad says it wouldn't be fair, because it couldn't live in Austin; we don't have a house there. We can't leave it here all alone, because we don't have anybody who'd take care of it when I wasn't around."

"Your dad's right. Having a dog is a big responsibility. They need to be taken care of every day. They need to be walked. They need to be fed. They need lots of playtime because they are full of energy, especially puppies. Plus, you have to make sure they get all their shots and give them medicine to make sure they don't get sick."

"I could do that." Daisy noted the rigid posture, the arms folded across his chest. She almost laughed at the stubborn set of his mouth, exactly like his father's. He was a typical boy with all the traits of one, gaining a hold on his personality and who he'd be as he got older. Derrick better be prepared, because he'd have his hands full with this guy when he hit his teen years.

"I bet you could. But would it be fair to the dog? I know

it's fun to play with dogs, throwing frisbees and balls for them to fetch. Training them to sit and roll over, and all the other cool stuff they can learn. Except what happens if you're only here for a weekend or two a month? He'd miss you like crazy, and probably be sad most of the time. It's a big responsibility, having a pet. It's why I don't have one. I work all the time, from early in the morning before the diner opens until it closes. I would feel bad if I couldn't go straight home and spend time with the dog."

"I guess that makes sense."

Derrick sat quietly through their conversation, and Daisy realized she might be stepping on somebody's toes, tossing her opinion in there like that.

"How is your uncle doing?" Derrick glanced her way before turning his attention back to the road.

"Uncle Joe is amazing. He's whipping around the house now that he's got that new motorized wheelchair. Plus, he's got a new online girlfriend, which amazes me, because six months ago the man didn't even know how to use Google."

"Good to hear it."

"He's also got buddies he plays poker with once or twice a week. I'm starting to think he's got a better social life than me."

Derrick glanced her way. "I know the feeling."

They drove in silence for several minutes, the radio playing softly, with the occasional sound of Ian's game in the background. It was nice because she rarely got driven anywhere. She did most of the heavy lifting at home. Uncle Joe did what he could, and she knew he felt guilty because there were things he couldn't do anymore. Going out to lunch, being chauffeured by Derrick, felt like pampering.

They pulled into the parking lot of the Italian restaurant, and everybody piled out of the car. Walking through the front door, Daisy inhaled deeply, loving the scent of tomato sauce and spices wafting through the air. It wasn't a high-end restaurant, but it wasn't a hole-in-the-wall, either. Families and couples were scattered at tables.

One of the things she liked was the bright sunlight pouring through big picture windows. She understood a lot of places used dimmer lighting to set a mood, an ambiance of intimacy, but she preferred to be able to see her food before and while eating it.

The hostess led them to a table toward the back, but not too close to the kitchen, and Derrick held out her chair. Their waitress handed them menus and left, coming back almost immediately with ice water and a basket of hot, fresh garlic bread. Her stomach growled as she inhaled the enticing aroma. In her rush to get to church, she'd grabbed a Pop Tart on her way out the door, and now she was starving.

After a quick perusal of the menu, she turned to Ian. "You're the expert. What do you recommend?"

He shrugged, putting his phone on the table. "They have good pizza. The lasagna's good, too."

"The lasagna is great." Derrick reached over and pointed

to something on the menu. "They also make a mean chicken piccata."

Ian shook his head. "Dad liked it. I didn't like those little green things. What were they called, Dad?"

"Capers."

"Yeah, they were gross."

"We have a rule. He has to try a food at least one time before he can say he doesn't like it. I've got the feeling capers are going to be one and done."

Daisy understood and approved of his rule. "I think that's a good idea. How do you know whether you'll like something or not unless you taste it?"

"Dad said he ate snails. Honest. He put slimy snails in his mouth and ate them." Ian shuddered, but looked at Daisy from behind his lashes, as if waiting to see her reaction.

"That's one of those foods that I made myself try too. I agree with Ian, yuck."

Derrick's laughter did funny things to her insides, and she laid a hand against her stomach. Ian laughed too, making her feel like part of the whole. She looked around the restaurant again, noticing there were many families seated among the patrons, mothers and fathers with kids. Booster seats seemed a norm in here, but for the most part, the children seemed well behaved and not overly rambunctious.

"You folks ready to order?"

Daisy smiled at the waitress, a redhead with the brightest

hair she'd ever seen, outside of a box of coloring. It was offset by a pair of startling blue eyes and a white smile. Probably in her early to mid-twenties, she had a charm and vivaciousness perfect for her job.

"I'd like the lasagna."

"We have meat or vegetarian."

"Definitely meat. Thanks." Daisy handed her the menu and spread her napkin across her lap.

"I'll have the same," Derrick added.

"I'll have the little pizza with pepperoni and extra cheese." Ian sat up straighter in his seat and handed her his menu. "Dad, can I have a soda?" At Derrick's nod, he added the soft drink to his order.

The waitress leaned down to talk softly with Ian, making sure to make eye contact with Derrick at the same time, a silent request for permission. "If it's okay with your dad, we open the game room in the back on Sundays."

Ian's eyes widened, and he sent a pleading look at his father. "Dad? Please?"

Derrick turned and looked toward the back of the restaurant, where several old-fashioned games lined the wall of their back room. There was a separate door sectioning it off from the rest of the restaurant, which explained why it wasn't blaring the sounds of bells and whistles throughout the place.

"Okay, but just until your food comes."

"Yes! Dad, you're the best!" Ian jumped from his chair,

ready to race toward the game room. Derrick held up his hand.

"Phone."

"Oops, sorry. I forgot." Ian grabbed his phone and shoved it in his pocket.

She watched him sprint toward the back room, his whole body seemed to vibrate with excitement. Derrick kept his eyes on his son the entire way until he'd made it through the opening.

"I know I'm being overprotective, but I'm new at this whole single parenting stuff. I make him keep his phone on him any time he's not with me. I want him to know I'm only a call away. Plus, if anything happens, I can track his phone's GPS."

"Smart dad."

Derrick took a sip of his water and set the glass down. "Educated dad. Hazard of the job, I guess."

"Makes me glad I run a restaurant. All I have to worry about is making sure the fresh produce is delivered on time."

He smiled at her lame joke and reached for her hand. "Daisy, I'm sorry. It seems like every time we've tried to get together, fate's conspired to throw a roadblock in our path. I'm starting to think—"

"Don't, Derrick. Some things aren't meant to happen. I've resigned myself to the fact we're not meant to be anything but friends. And I'm okay with that. In fact, it's probably better. I don't have the best track record with

DERRICK

relationships."

Squeezing her hand, he gave a bitter-sounding laugh. "Welcome to my world. The longest relationship I've ever had was with my ex-wife, and that only lasted a couple of years. Mind you, I'll never regret it because it gave me Ian."

"Which makes you a very lucky man."

Inside, she was breaking apart, because she'd secretly hoped they might be willing to take a chance. This was probably best, though, because it wouldn't have worked. Even though Austin wasn't that far away in terms of miles, they'd still be living separate lives, because Derrick's job kept him in the city, and she'd never leave Shiloh Springs. It had become her haven, her safe place, the one spot where she finally felt grounded. Her whole life she'd been rootless, searching for something, someone to give her purpose, and she'd found that at Daisy's Diner.

"I love my son. He's the best part of me. But his life has been turned upside down, and right now, he needs me. I can't be selfish, no matter how much I want it to be otherwise. But I want you to know, if things were different, I'd find a way to make us work."

"Dad, those games are so cool." Ian slid onto his chair, practically bouncing with enthusiasm and energy.

"We'll have to check them out later. Looks like our food's here." With a final squeeze, he turned her hand loose, and Daisy immediately missed his touch, the warmth which spread through her when he'd leaned in close. But she had to acknowledge he was right. Anything more than friendship between them was asking too much. Especially with her past.

Oh, but she'd had dreams. Dreams which now tasted like ashes in her mouth, leaving behind the bitter taste of defeat.

Pasting on a smile, she fought back tears and picked up her fork. Might as well enjoy their last meal together before they headed back to Austin.

CHAPTER FIVE

Monday morning came far too early for Derrick. After driving home from Shiloh Springs, he and Ian stopped for greasy hamburgers and fries through the fast-food drive-thru along with chocolate shakes, and plopped in front of the television, doing a superhero movie marathon. This morning, he had an up-too-late headache and was nursing his second cup of coffee.

"Ian, you gotta get up and get ready for school."

When only silence answered him, he eased from the chair at the tiny kitchen set and headed down the hallway. Pushing open the bedroom door to his son's room, he found Ian already dressed and stuffing dirty clothes into his hamper. Wonder of wonders, he could actually see the hardwood floors. It was a miracle because he hadn't seen them since Ian moved in.

"Hey, kiddo, what do you want for breakfast?"

Ian looked at Derrick, his blue eyes shining. "Cereal's okay."

"I can make you something. I can cook, you know?" When Ian simply looked at him without saying a word,

Derrick conceded. "Fine, cereal works for me. Five minutes. Good job, by the way. I'll put them in the washer before I head to the office."

"Can you teach me how to do it? I need to be…responsible…for helping out, right?

"Of course I'll teach you."

"Cool."

Derrick gave his son one final glance, almost convinced aliens had abducted his real kid and replaced him with a pod person. Wanting to learn to do laundry? Wanting to be more responsible? Definitely wasn't the same child who'd barely raised his backside from the sofa long enough to go to the bathroom or to eat.

In the kitchen, he grabbed the box of cereal and dumped some into a bowl, hoping the sugary concoction wouldn't rot Ian's teeth, and put the carton of milk and a spoon on the table. Reaching into the fridge, he pulled out one of the individual boxes of apple juice and sat it next to the bowl. Best he could do.

Ian ambled into the kitchen and sat in the chair across from Derrick and poured milk into the bowl until the cereal practically drowned in the stuff. He started shoveling it in, barely pausing to swallow in between bites.

"Slow down. You've got time before the bus gets here."

"Sorry. I'm starving."

Derrick almost shuddered at the thought of anything more than coffee going into his stomach. He was still feeling the aftereffects of their fast-food splurge from the night before. Ah, to be young enough to enjoy all the joys of living and doing anything you want without repercussions. Watching his son, enveloped in the glow of being a kid, having his whole life ahead of him, made Derrick suddenly feel old.

"So, what do you think about Ms. Patti trying to get us the house we looked at yesterday?"

"Which one?"

Derrick was tempted to bang his head against the tabletop. They'd talked about both houses on the drive home. Again in between movies. Now, it was like nothing had stuck in his kid's brain.

"You said you liked the blue one best. Did you change your mind?"

Ian shook his head and shoveled another mouthful of cereal in. "It was okay. No pool, but there was one at the place. I forgot what she called it."

"Activities center. Yeah, that one had the community pool. Might be nice; you can meet other kids your age there."

"I like the house. With the extra bedroom, you can have an office."

"I don't know, maybe we can come up with something fun to use that extra bedroom for. I'm hoping I don't need a whole office. That's why we're getting a place in Shiloh Springs, so that I can get away from working all the time, right?"

Ian laid his spoon inside the bowl and sat back, his head hung down where Derrick couldn't see his eyes.

"I wasn't sure if that's what you really wanted. I know you have lots of work. People counting on you. I—I don't want you to lose your job because you have me."

Derrick rose and walked around to squat beside his son, wrapping his arm around his shoulder. He'd hoped Ian had realized he wasn't going anywhere, that he'd always be there for him, no matter what. Guess he had a lot more work to do, convincing his son he'd always be around.

"Ian, I love you. It doesn't matter how many people are counting on me or if I lose my job. You are more important than any of that. You will always—*always*—be the most important thing in my life. We are in this together. Nobody gives up. Nobody leaves. Whatever life throws at us, we handle it together. You and me against the world. Got it?"

Ian's body shook beneath his hand, and he was surprised when his son swiveled in his seat and threw his arms around Derrick's neck, burrowing his face in the crook of his shoulder. He felt the wetness of his son's tears against his skin.

"Mom left." Ian's voice broke, his whispered words nearly rending Derrick's heart in two.

"Mom leaving was not your fault, Ian. You did nothing wrong. Sometimes people need a break to figure out things. That's what happened with your mom. It doesn't mean she doesn't love you, because she does."

"Okay." His sniffled response made Derrick want to hunt down his ex for breaking his kid's heart. Except what could he do once he found her? She'd made her choice when she'd signed away all parental rights, a fact he planned to never reveal to his son.

"Go wash your face and grab your backpack, the bus will be here soon."

When Ian bounded down the hall, he rinsed the dishes and put them in the dishwasher. He filled a travel mug with coffee because he had the feeling it was going to be a long day.

When Ian reappeared with a clean face and freshly brushed teeth, he grabbed his briefcase and hat, and they headed for the bus stop. He'd call Ms. Patti from the office and tell her to put in an offer. The sooner he got a place in Shiloh Springs, the sooner Ian would feel begin to feel safe and loved. Hopefully.

"Good morning, Miss Edna," Daisy called from the foyer of Creekside Inn, Shiloh Spring's bed and breakfast. She made it a point to check in on the owner, not just as a neighbor but because she genuinely liked the older woman.

"I'm in the kitchen, Daisy, come on back."

Daisy smiled at the deep, baritone-sounding woman's

voice peeling from across the space. From a lifetime of smoking, Miss Edna's voice was gruff and gravely sounding, but louder than anybody else Daisy knew. She could be mistaken for a lighthouse foghorn in volume.

She found Miss Edna standing at the oven, pulling out a tray of biscuits. The smell wafting through the kitchen had Daisy smiling. There was something about the smell of freshly baked biscuits that appealed to her on a cerebral level. The endorphins gave her a happy feeling.

"Those smell wonderful, Miss Edna. Your tenants are lucky to have you cooking for them."

"Pull up a chair, honey. I just need to put these out on the sideboard, and then we can sit and have some coffee."

She wrapped the hot, fresh biscuits in a napkin-lined basket and carried them into the glass-enclosed sunroom off the kitchen, where guests were treated to a buffet-style breakfast. The lovely Victorian home that housed the B&B contained several guest suites, as well as a couple that had been converted to long-term apartments. Miss Edna always had somebody coming and going, keeping the older woman busy and happy, though Daisy wondered how much longer she'd be able to manage things on her own.

When she shuffled back into the kitchen, Daisy couldn't help noticing she seemed a little bit unsteady on her feet and couldn't help thinking that getting older wasn't for the faint of heart. Especially with somebody like Miss Edna, who didn't have any close family she could count on.

Reaching into the cupboard, she pulled down a couple of small plates and carried them to the table, sitting one in front of Daisy, and another at the empty seat beside her. She shuffled back across the kitchen space, picked up a second basket of hot biscuits and the coffee pot, and brought them to the table.

Daisy had to hold onto the side of her chair to keep from jumping up and helping Miss Edna, but they'd had this argument so many times she could have recited it by heart. Miss Edna didn't want the help, she wanted—no, needed— to do things for herself. To be independent and self-sufficient. She'd told Daisy more than once when she stopped being able to take care of her guests, she'd close the place down, rather than have somebody else waiting on her hand and foot.

"Butter and honey already on the table. Fix yourself up a biscuit while they're hot."

Daisy loaded on the honey and the butter and took a bite, moaning as she savored the buttery goodness. How was it possible that every time she had one of Miss Edna's biscuits, it tasted better than the one before?

"It's always a joy to see you enjoying my cooking. Makes it worthwhile."

"I will never turn down your biscuits, Miss Edna. I've tried and tried the recipe you gave me, and they still turn out like hockey pucks."

"You're probably overmixing the dough. Are you freezing

the butter before you use it?" At Daisy's nod, because she had her mouth full, she continued. "Cold buttermilk, too?"

"Yes, ma'am. I just don't have your touch."

Miss Edna's barking laugh could probably be heard all the way into town, but it warmed Daisy's heart. Under her frail exterior beat the heart of a warrior, which was probably why so many people underestimated her. Being older didn't mean she'd lost a step intellectually, and she often came to Miss Edna for advice when she ran into problems at the diner.

"How's that fella of yours, Daisy? The boy of his is like a smaller version of his daddy."

"Why does everybody think Derrick and I are together? He comes into the diner to eat when he's in Shiloh Springs. We tried a couple of times to go out, but something always interfered. We have had one—count them—one meal together, which was yesterday. And his son came with us, so you can't really call it a date."

"Mark my words, young lady, he's smitten. If he's bringing his son to meet you, well, in my day that meant something."

Daisy's breath caught in her throat at the thought, but immediately dismissed the image. Derrick had brought Ian with him because they were looking for a place to live, not to meet her. The notion was ridiculous—wasn't it?

"Derrick and Ian were here looking for a place for long weekends and holidays. Someplace to get away from the hustle and bustle of Austin when they've got the chance. It has nothing to do with me."

"That man is looking for a place to plant roots. A place to raise his son, true, but he's looking for more. He's looking to have his heart healed, with somebody he can trust. I think he sees in you a person he can trust, not only with his son, but with his soul. Think you're up to the task?"

"Miss Edna, this is an awfully deep conversation to be having over biscuits and coffee. Besides, I have to get to the diner. I'm already running late, and Ike's gonna bite my head off." Standing up, she walked over and placed a quick kiss against the leathery cheek skin of her friend.

"I love you to pieces, Miss Edna, and I mean this in the nicest way possible. Mind your own business."

Giving her a quick wink, Daisy left, leaving the other woman laughing her head off behind her. She quickly walked the distance between the B&B and the house she shared with her uncle, which was across the street and down about four houses on the right.

Doing a quick check on her uncle, she climbed behind the wheel of her yellow Bug and drove to the diner, ready to start her morning. Good thing she could drive the route by heart, because her head was filled with the words Miss Edna spoke, repeating over and over.

Shaking her head at her nonsensical thoughts, she focused her mind on what she could handle, the diner and her regulars, the people who made her life worthwhile.

CHAPTER SIX

It was another two weeks before Derrick managed to get back to Shiloh Springs. After some astounding negotiation by Ms. Patti, he had reached an agreement to buy the house and get an early closing. In his pocket was the check for the final closing costs and the title company, and everything was done except for the signing. He wasn't sure how Ms. Patti had worked her magic, but he was grateful because Ian had gotten downright surly. Maybe getting into a place of his own, that sense of stability, of being able to decorate his room anyway he wanted with his own furniture, might make him feel like he belonged.

"We're almost there. Can you believe it? Today's the day. Once we sign the papers, the house belongs to us. Lock, stock, and hefty mortgage payments."

Silence met him. Ian had withdrawn in the past couple of weeks and had become a moody, snarky, and sullen facsimile of the boy he'd been just two weeks ago when they'd been in Shiloh Springs. He hoped being back in the small town would invoke a spark of the son he'd been before.

"What's the first thing you want to do once we've got the

keys?"

"I don't know."

"Come on, Ian. Aren't you a little bit excited? We're starting a new adventure."

When Ian simply shrugged, Derrick was sorely tempted to pull the truck over to the side of the road and shake him. Why couldn't he see this was a new start for them both? A chance to learn and grow closer, and be a real family?

"Can we go to the diner after?"

"Sure can. I bet Daisy will be excited to hear about the new house."

"Maybe."

Guess that's the best I'm gonna get. Better than nothing. I wish I could figure out how to get through to him. My own son, and most of the time it's like I'm talking to a stranger.

It took longer than Derrick expected to deal with all the paperwork and hand over the gigantic check. His savings had taken a huge hit, but it would be worth it. Something about having his own piece of Shiloh Springs felt right. He couldn't describe what the feeling was, but it started deep in his gut and traveled straight to his chest. Warmth and a feeling of connection, of being part of a greater whole. And didn't that sound like a sappy greeting card?

Pulling up in front of the diner, he jockeyed for a parking space. Looked like business was booming in downtown Shiloh Springs today. Since it was a Saturday morning, it wasn't surprising.

"Hope we can find a table. Looks like everybody's wanting to eat out today."

"We can come back. I mean, if you want."

Derrick couldn't hide his smile. "Let's see if they've got an open table. If not, we'll come back."

"Because you want to see Daisy, right?" Ian's smirk was a sight to see, the twinkle in his blue eyes something Derrick had missed seeing. When was the last time he'd seen it? Oh, yeah, two weeks ago—when they'd gone to the Italian place with Daisy.

"I think you're the one who's looking forward to seeing Daisy again."

"She's okay."

High praise indeed, my son.

Walking through the front doors, the noise level was overwhelming. Almost every seat was taken. Just as Derrick was getting ready to turn around and leave, he spotted Rafe Boudreau and his brother, Brody, seated at a table toward the back. A third place setting was on the table, so he suspected somebody else would be showing up.

Rafe raised his hand and motioned then over. Placing his hands on Ian's shoulders, he steered his son toward Rafe's table.

"Momma said you'd be in town today. Congratulations on your new house."

"Thanks. Just came from signing the paperwork and handing over a disgustingly large check. Picked up the keys and thought we'd stop here and celebrate."

"Congratulations, Williamson. Looks like we're gonna be neighbors." Antonio strolled over toward them and clapped Derrick on the back. He liked the other man. He was a solid worker, with a quick brain and an even temper. They worked well together, and was probably the primary reason he'd even considered Shiloh Springs. Antonio Boudreau had been the reason he'd first visited, working a case concerning the woman who was now Antonio's wife.

"Can I go talk to Daisy?" Ian pointed over to where Daisy stood behind the counter, ringing up a customer. She smiled when she caught his stare, her face lit with an inner joy few people had.

"For a minute. Don't bother her if she's too busy though, okay?"

Ian nodded and made his way over to Daisy, who enveloped him in a big hug. The funny thing was, Ian hugged her back.

"You got a minute, Williamson? Would like to pick your brain about something." Rafe pointed to the empty chair. "Daisy will keep an eye on your boy for a couple minutes."

Derrick sat in the empty chair, which gave him a clear view of the counter, where his son slid onto an empty vinyl-covered stool. He couldn't help noticing that his son was talking a mile a minute to Daisy. Seeing his son this animated had him catching his breath, overcome with emotion. Just about everything he'd tried to bring his son out of his self-imposed shell hadn't worked. If anything, he'd retreated further away. But less than five minutes in Daisy's presence, and he was a chatterbox.

"Looks like you've got competition for Daisy's heart."

Derrick swung his attention to Rafe, who'd made the offhanded comment. "What?"

Rafe nodded toward Ian. "He's found a soulmate in her, a kindred spirit. It'll do him good to be around her. She's got a heart as big as Texas."

"He did want to see her after we signed the paperwork."

"All the young'uns around here adore her. She has a special ability, a knack, of making them feel…" He snapped his fingers. "What's the word I'm looking for?"

"Cherished," Brody and Antonio answered at the same time.

Derrick drew in a deep breath, glancing toward his son again. "He could use a little—actually a lot—of feeling special right now. This whole thing with his mom, it's hit him hard, but he doesn't want to talk about it. I'm considering getting him counseling because I'm not sure what to do next."

"You've already made the first step in the right direction, man. He needs time and he needs to know that no matter what, you're going to be there for the long haul. Don't worry, Shiloh Springs will be good for Ian, wait and see."

Daisy felt Ian's arms slide around her waist, his hug surprising. He practically vibrated with excitement and his grin was infectious.

"Guess what?"

"No clue. What's going on?" She smiled indulgently, wanting to reach forward and brush the hair off his forehead.

"We bought a house. Dad signed the papers this morning, and Ms. Patti gave us keys and everything. It doesn't have a pool, but that's okay because pools are a lot of work. Ms. Patti told me that it takes chemicals and stuff all the time, and if you don't take really good care of them, they turn all green and gross, and stuff starts growing in them."

"Ms. Patti is absolutely right. Plus, all that green stuff gets slimy and icky." Daisy leaned forward conspiratorially and whispered, "And it stinks. Pew."

Ian's laughter felt like a balm to her soul. The last time she'd seen him a couple weeks earlier, he'd been withdrawn, and getting him to talk when they'd gone out to eat had been like pulling hen's teeth.

"You're funny."

"I've been told that a time or two. You and your dad staying for lunch?"

Ian nodded. "Rafe wanted to talk to Dad about something. Work, I guess." He spun around on the stool and pointed toward his dad, who was in an animated conversation with Rafe and his brothers. "He's always working."

"Well, then, I'll check on him in a minute. In the meantime, what can I get you?"

"I don't know. I wasn't hungry before, but…"

"Now you're starving." Daisy touched a finger to the side of her nose. "It's Ike's cooking. One whiff and your tummy will start growling. Today's special is meatloaf, if you're interested."

"Cool. Does it have mashed potatoes?"

Daisy feigned shock, a hand placed dramatically to her chest. "Does it come with mashed potatoes? What, do you think we're heathens around here? Who doesn't eat mashed potatoes with their meatloaf? Ike makes an awesome gravy to go with them, too."

"We'll take two, one for me and one for Dad."

"Coming right up, sir. And since you're celebrating the new house, how about a milkshake to go with your meal?"

"Strawberry?"

She smiled and ruffled his hair, unable to resist his cuteness another second. "I knew there was a reason I liked you. Strawberry's my jam, too."

At his answering grin, she knew she'd given the right answer. Filling out the ticket, she put in the order and moved to the cash register, and checked out another satisfied customer, judging by the size of the tip.

She made the rounds, refilling water glasses, and topping off other drinks. Within minutes, she found herself standing beside Derrick, still seated at the table with the Boudreaus. When he looked up, a slow smile had the creases in his cheeks standing out. She so rarely saw those cute dimples, her heart fluttered in her chest, and she felt flustered. Darn it, she was a grown woman, not a teenager with her first crush. So how was he able to make her feel like a giggling schoolgirl?

"Afternoon, Daisy. I guess Ian told you we signed on the new house?"

"He did. He seems pretty happy about it, even if it doesn't have a pool."

"Trust me, we had more than one discussion on the pros and cons of having a pool. I think the extra work clinched the deal. Besides, he's talking about reading up on gardening."

She handed him the glass of sweet tea in her hand. "Let me know if he needs any help with that. Or he can talk to Rafe. He's got a green thumb and can grow just about anything."

"Hmm. Good idea." Derrick chuckled when Rafe rolled his eyes, while Antonio and Brody laughed like loons.

"By the way, Ian ordered lunch for you. It should be out in a couple minutes."

"He did?"

"Yep." She leaned in a little, speaking softly. "I think you'll like it."

"I'm sure I will. Do you mind letting him sit at the counter? I don't want him making a pest of himself."

"Don't you dare! Ian is a true joy, and he's more than

welcome to sit at the counter anytime."

Derrick held his hands up in surrender, and Daisy wondered if she'd overreacted. Probably. She didn't like anybody regarding their kids like they were an imposition or unwanted. They didn't know how lucky they were to have those irreplaceable blessings.

"I'll be back with your lunch."

She moved to the next table and took their order before heading back to the kitchen. Quickly picking up the two plates, she deposited one in front of Ian and watched him dig in, a huge piece of meatloaf disappearing into his mouth. Chewing, he gave her a thumb's up.

Carrying the other plate across the diner, she placed it in front of Derrick, watching him closely for his reaction. The slow curve of his smile did dangerous things to her insides, and she swallowed down her sudden nervousness.

"My son ordered this for me?"

"Surprised?"

He looked down at the plate again, then nodded, his eyes twinkling with unsuppressed mirth.

"I figured he'd get a hamburger and fries. Or his usual chicken and dumplings. But meatloaf? I didn't even know he liked it."

Daisy leaned in closer and whispered, "I think it was the mashed potatoes that sold him."

"Gotcha. Add mashed potatoes to my repertoire."

Only then did she noticed that the Boudreaus he'd been

sitting with earlier were gone and he was alone at the table.

"Get through all your business? I can send Ian over here if you'd like."

"Let him stay at the counter if he wants. This is the happiest I've seen him in days. He's been distant and moody ever since we were here the last time. Just between you and me, I'm worried about him."

"Change is always hard. As adults, we learn to adapt and deal with what life throws at us—the good, the bad, and the ugly. Kids haven't learned the coping mechanisms they need to process dramatic upheavals. Be patient but set some boundaries." She paused and placed a hand softly on his shoulder, squeezing it gently. "You're a good dad. You've proved that by noticing he's hurting and wanting to help."

"Thanks, Daisy. I needed to hear that today."

"Well, dig in. If you need anything, holler. I've got hungry customers to deal with." She smiled at him and turned to walk back to the kitchen area. "By the way, congratulations again on the new house."

"Thanks. As soon as we get some furniture and stuff, we'd love to have you over. I'm sure Ian will want to show you his new digs."

"It's a date. Let me know when, and I'll be there."

She placed a hand on her stomach to quiet the quivers rioting inside her. Had she really just called it a date? Was she insane? As much as she liked Derrick, nothing could come of getting involved with him. Too much baggage to bring into any relationship, it wasn't worth the risk of getting her heart broken.

With a sigh, she picked up the next order, wishing she could change the past—because if Derrick ever found out the truth, she'd have more to worry about than just a broken heart.

CHAPTER SEVEN

"I'm sorry, kiddo. The furniture store can't get the stuff delivered for two more days. They said that's only because they're putting a rush on the order, or we'd be waiting another week."

"What are we gonna do if we don't have beds? Sleep on the floor?"

Derrick looked around the empty living room of their new house. The hardwood floors gleamed to a high shine. The open floor plan opened to a staircase, leading to the bedrooms upstairs when you walked in the front door. To the right was what Ms. Patti called the formal living room. On the other side of the staircase were the family room and kitchen. A large stone fireplace on the far wall would be great for winter time and the holidays. He found himself looking forward to Christmas with Ian, something he hadn't been able to do when he'd lived with his mother.

"I don't know about you, but I'm not sleeping on the floor. How about we head over to the B&B and see if Miss Edna can put us up for the next night or two? Comfy beds and sausage and biscuits for breakfast sounds better than sleeping on hardwood floors and fast-food drive-through cardboard breakfast, right?"

"I guess." Ian scuffed his sneaker-clad foot against the floor. "What are we gonna do about school? If we stay for two more days, I'm going to miss classes."

"Don't worry. I'll call and make sure the school knows. It'll be an excused absence. You haven't missed much, so everything's gonna be fine."

When his answer was met with silence, Derrick studied Ian, noting his slumped shoulders and resigned expression. After he'd been so enthusiastic earlier at the diner, he hoped they'd turned a corner. Now it seemed they'd taken two steps backward. And he had no idea how to make things better.

"Are you—never mind."

"What? You can ask me anything."

Ian walked across the living room and lifted one of the slats in the blinds and looked outside. "Are you gonna be working while we're here? It's okay if you have to."

Reading between the lines, Derrick knew that it was anything but okay. Was his son feeling neglected? He'd already cut back on his hours, as much as he could anything. Heading the Austin office wasn't exactly an eight-to-five job.

"I don't plan on working. This is our time, you and me, bud. It's a little too cold for swimming, but maybe we use some of the other things at the clubhouse. Shoot some hoops. How's that sound?"

At Ian's enthusiastic nod, Derrick made a promise to make time to spend doing activities with him. Think about setting something up in the backyard they could do together.

"Alright, let's get settled into the B&B and change clothes. We can head over to the clubhouse after that."

Pulling out his phone, he quickly dialed the B&B. Miss Edna assured him they were welcome and could stay as long as needed. One problem solved. Now, to figure out the complex puzzle that was a nine-year-old boy.

Daisy carried the heavy-laden tray to the table filled with visitors. From their brief conversation, they were visiting friends in Santa Lucia, which wasn't far away, just over the county line. Their friends mentioned Shiloh Springs and recommended they stop at Daisy's place when they were going through town. They'd had a million questions about her, the diner, the town, and the townsfolk. Normally she'd have been happy to oblige their small talk, but seeing it was the weekend, she'd been slammed pretty much all morning and early afternoon.

After unloading the tray, she did stay and answer a few more questions about their town, because she loved Shiloh Springs and everything about it. One of the best decisions of her life was when she'd left her old life behind and moved back to help Uncle Joe run the diner. As far as she was concerned, she never planned on living anywhere else ever again.

After another half hour or so of nonstop orders, things finally started slowing and she was able to draw in a deep breath. Looking around the place, she wondered what others saw when they walked in the door. Over the past couple of years, she made some changes, mostly minor and cosmetic, but they gave the place a modern yet nostalgic vibe. Booths lined two of the walls, including seating beside the big picture window with the diner's name emblazoned in big letters.

When the bell over the door tinkled, she glanced up, smiling when she spotted her friends. Serena, Tessa, and Beth walked in and made a beeline for one of the open tables. Daisy didn't say a word when they grabbed another nearby table and pulled it over, lining it up with the table they'd chosen, making a bigger seating area. Guess they were expecting company.

"Afternoon, ladies."

"Hi, Daisy. We've got a couple more coming. Hope you don't mind my pushiness in moving your stuff around."

"Not a problem. You saved me the trouble. How many are we waiting for?"

"Camilla's here, so she's coming. Also, Nica's home. Not sure if Ms. Patti will make it or not. She said she'd stop by if she finished up early with her clients."

"So five, maybe six. Do y'all need menus or do you know

what you want?"

"Menus? We don't need no stinking menus." Beth's lips curled upward when she quoted the famous line. Daisy chuckled at her bad, over-the-top accent.

Before she could shoot back a reply, the bell over the door sounded again, and she spotted Nica Boudreau entering. The perky blond hadn't been home in a while, much to Ms. Patti's consternation. She'd been finishing up her senior year of college, having finished one master's degree and working on a second. Nobody worked harder than Nica at achieving her goals, and Daisy admired the heck out of her. Though she personally hadn't had the luxury or wherewithal to advance her own education, she knew the lone Boudreau daughter had her future planned out, and never deviated or strayed far from the path. She envied that kind of dedication and determination.

"Daisy!" Nica gave Daisy a quick hug, her smile ticking up the corners of her mouth. "Long time, no see."

"I wondered when you'd be darkening my doors again. If I'd know, I'd have had Ike make some of his five-alarm chili you like so much. Extra spicy with enough of a kick to set the drapes on fire."

"This is just an unplanned visit. Got homesick and need-ed to feel the dirt of the Big House between my toes. School's fine and all, but there's nothing like coming home, being around family, to help ground your soul."

"Well, y'all sit. I'll be back with water and sweet tea in a second."

It didn't take long for her to pass out glasses filled with sweet tea. She returned with a full pitcher, leaving it on their table, so they could refill their glasses instead of waiting. While the crowd had started to clear, there were still customers who needed tending. Besides, it was time for Jackie to head home. Turned out, she'd been a godsend, and fit in well with Ike. As long as she wanted to work at the diner, she'd have a job.

She glanced up when she caught movement from the corner of her eye and spotted Heath and Camilla outside the big picture window. Heath had pulled Camilla into a passionate embrace, kissing her like he never wanted to let her go. Fortunately, Camilla didn't look like she wanted to be anywhere else than in his arms. When they broke apart, Heath spotted Daisy watching and waved, giving her a wink. Camilla swatted him playfully before turning and walking through the front door. Heath walked down the sidewalk, probably headed toward the sheriff's office to visit with his brother.

"Sorry I'm late." Camilla slid onto an empty chair and picked up a glass of water, rubbing it against her forehead. "I was unavoidably detained."

When the other ladies laughed, Daisy got the impression this wasn't an unusual situation with Camilla and Heath. Immediately, her mind flew to thoughts of Derrick, and she felt heat rush into her face.

Stop it. Never gonna happen, girl. Daydreams and wishes can't change reality. Let it go.

"Good to see you, Camilla. How's the move going?"

"We've almost got everything lined up, Daisy. Everything back in North Carolina is packed. The movers are scheduled. My place is sold. I'll have to head back long enough for the closing, and any last-minute stuff, but otherwise, in two weeks I'll be a permanent resident of Shiloh Springs."

"How's Heath settling into working from Austin? I know it has to be a big change from all the frenetic energy of Washington D.C."

"He's loving it. And his office is thrilled to have somebody with his experience. All in all, everything's working out for both of us. I can write anywhere, as long as I've got Wi-Fi and a laptop. Speaking of, the new book comes out next month."

Daisy grinned. "I know. I've already got it pre-ordered, so it'll be on my e-reader the minute it's available."

"Me, too!" A chorus of female voices echoed Daisy's. Camilla blushed at their words.

"Alright, ladies. Now that we've embarrassed the new girl, how about I take your orders?"

"Any recommendations?" Camilla looked at Daisy, a question in her gaze.

"Ike made pot roast today with potatoes, carrots, and brown gravy. Homemade yeast rolls."

Every hand at the table raised, and Daisy felt a surge of emotion well up deep inside. Knowing these ladies, her friends, trusted her suggestion made her feel almost like she was a part of their group. Oh, she wasn't really an outsider, having a deep friendship with every one of them, but that wasn't the same as being an intimate part of the Boudreau clan. Of course, since all of the Boudreau men were like brothers to her, anything more than friendship would have been icky.

"Got it. Let me get these orders to Ike. It'll be out in a few minutes. Let me know if y'all need anything."

Less than five minutes later, Ike had their orders ready, and she delivered them to the table. Placing two baskets of rolls in the middle of the table, she started to turn away and head for the kitchen.

"Hold it right there, girlfriend. You're not getting away that easy," Tessa's voice teased, and Daisy spun around, brow quirked.

"What? Did I forget something?"

"Yes. You haven't told us how things are going with you and Derrick Williamson."

Daisy threw her hands in the air. "Why is everybody asking me that? There isn't a 'me and Derrick'."

"Yet," Serena added, her eyes sparkling with laughter.

Daisy crossed her arms over her chest, glaring at the women. "I want to know who started this rumor, because I need to nip it in the bud."

They each looked at the other and with one voice answered, "Momma Boudreau!"

Daisy's scream echoed through the diner because she knew she'd been defeated by an expert.

Because when Ms. Patti spoke, it might as well be written in stone. She just hoped Derrick didn't hear about this.

CHAPTER EIGHT

Ian instinctively knew what his dad was about to say before he'd even opened his mouth. Honestly, he'd been expecting it anyway, so he couldn't claim to be surprised. Except he was. Surprised and ticked off. Because he'd promised—no work. This was supposed to be *their* time together.

"I'm sorry, Ian. Rafe needs help from the FBI and it's not right for somebody to have to come from Austin when I'm already here."

"But it's not fair. You promised this was our time. Now you're going to work, and there's nothing for me to do."

"Come on…"

"No, you come on. Whenever you say we'll do something, we never do. Work always comes first."

He felt a horrible burning pain in the middle of his chest, red hot and growing. It happened more and more lately, making him want to throw things. Break something. Scream at the top of his lungs until he couldn't scream anymore. Balling his hands into fists at his sides, he fought down the urge to punch his dad hard. Make him understand how bad he hurt inside.

"We can still go to the clubhouse. As soon as I get back, we'll head over."

"Forget it. It's not important anyway. Go help the sheriff."

"Ian—"

"I understand, Dad. I'm mad, okay? I'm being a jerk. Just go. Like you always tell me, the faster you go, the faster you'll get back."

His dad sighed, and Ian knew deep down he was being a brat and making his dad feel bad. It wasn't his dad's fault that everybody needed him. His dad worked hard. Sometimes he'd wake up and see his dad's light on. More than once, he'd tiptoed down the hall and saw him working on his computer while Ian had been asleep.

"Promise me you'll stay here. I already talked to Miss Edna, and she'll keep an eye on you. Do not leave the B&B for any reason. Keep your cell phone with you, so I can check up on you while I'm gone. Do not—"

He rolled his eyes, and barely contained a scream. "Dad, I know the rules. Don't talk to strangers. Don't take anything to eat or drink from anybody you don't approve of. Don't go outside. Don't leave the property. I'm not a baby."

"No, you're not. You're so grown up it scares me. Sometimes—doing what I do, seeing the kinds of people I have to arrest—it scares me something bad might happen to you. So I tend to be overly cautious. That's what dads do."

Ian dropped his chin to his chest, feeling like a jerk. Hearing his dad talk about the bad people he dealt with every day, could he blame him for wanting to catch the bad guys and keep people safe? It wasn't like he was leaving him behind in Shiloh Springs and heading back to Austin without him.

"I get it, Dad. I promise. Go help Rafe catch the bad guys, and then we'll go shoot hoops. I've got my games, I can keep busy."

"Thank you. When I get back, we'll do whatever you want, promise."

It felt good when his dad pulled him in for a hug, but the burning anger in his chest hadn't gone away, not really, but the white-hot fury that consumed him earlier had faded. Guess he'd better get used to the feeling, because he doubted things would change. Not really.

"Phone on you at all times, got it?"

Reaching into his pocket, he pulled his phone out and held it up to show his dad. Sheesh, he wasn't stupid enough to leave his phone. Sometimes he forgot to charge it, but he never left it anywhere.

When his dad pulled him into a headlock and started scrubbing his hand over his hair, he struggled to get loose, giggling the whole time. Twisting in his dad's arms, he felt his father's fingers digging into his sides, tickling him, and he wiggled and shifted, laughing so hard he lost his breath.

Finally, when he couldn't take another second of it, he

was free, his father's grin making everything better.

"Be good. Don't give Miss Edna any problems."

"I will. I won't. I mean, I'll be good, and I won't give Miss Edna any difficulty."

"See you in a bit, kiddo."

"Yeah, yeah. Get lost, old man."

His dad chuckled at his words, and within seconds, he was out the front door, leaving Ian behind.

Plopping down on one of the chairs in the lobby, he laid his phone on the arm of the chair and took out his video game, immediately pulling up his character and started killing zombie hoards.

He wasn't sure how much time passed, but when his stomach growled, he decided to see if Miss Edna had any snacks. Cookies would be good right about now. Or cake. He hadn't had cake since the piece he'd shared in the diner with his dad. And he loved cake, especially German chocolate. All the gooey coconut and pecans on top? Yum. While he wasn't super strict, his dad didn't keep a lot of junk food in his condo, so Ian didn't get nearly the sugar rush he used to get living with his mom. She always had sweets around. Claimed she was a chocaholic and needed to get her fix when the urge struck. Ian reaped the benefits of always having sugary treats available. Sometimes he wondered if he missed his mom's lax attitude about everything more than he missed her.

Setting his game next to his phone on the arm of the

chair, he headed to the kitchen and found Miss Edna unloading the dishwasher. Without a word, he pitched in over her protests. It wasn't much work to put dishes into cupboards, and he didn't mind helping. Especially since Miss Edna was old, like really old, and couldn't get around so good.

"Thank you, Ian. As my momma used to say, many hands make light work."

Ian's brow scrunched up. "What's that mean?"

Miss Edna smiled and handed him the cookie jar without him even having to ask for anything. "It means when people work together, the job gets done faster and isn't as hard as doing it alone."

"That makes sense."

"Help yourself to some cookies. Growing boys need to eat lots. It helps them grow big and strong."

Ian looked down at his thin frame. "It'll take a lot of cookies to make me bigger."

Miss Edna patted his hand. "Trust me, you're going to wind up as big as your dad, maybe bigger. You might be small now, but you've got good bones. When your growth spurt hits, you're gonna be like one of those lone oaks. Strong and sturdy and immovable."

"I'd like that." Because he hated being the small kid in class. He either got picked on or ignored. Sometimes being invisible wasn't a bad thing.

"Want some milk with those cookies?"

Ian nodded, taking another bite. These snickerdoodles tasted good. He liked the cinnamon and sugar on the outside. A glass of milk appeared on the table in front of him, and he thanked Miss Edna around a mouthful of cookie.

"Can I ask you something?"

"Of course."

"Why is the B&B named The Creekside Inn? We've stayed here a couple times, and I haven't seen any creeks."

Miss Edna chuckled and lots of lines crinkled out from the corners of her eyes. Like the ones his mom used to call laugh lines. Guess Miss Edna did a lot of laughing, coz she sure had a lot of them.

"There is a creek, but it's not exactly close anymore. Did you know that rivers and creeks can change their courses over lots of years? When the house was first built, the creek ran behind it. Never close, but it was fresh water for the gardens and kept the land lush and green. Over the years, things like erosion, flooding, and the speed of the water all worked together until the creek is much farther away now than it used to be."

"It's still out there?" Ian took a big swig of his milk and wiped his mouth on the back of his forearm.

"Oh, yes. It's not one of the bigger ones, like the one running through the Boudreau ranch, but it's still out there."

Miss Edna stood and pointed toward the back of the B&B, where there were lots of tall trees, almost looking like a forest, visible through the large glass windows. Even squinting, he couldn't make out anything that looked like water.

"I used to head over to the creek on the really hot days. Course, I was younger then." She chuckled before adding, "Nowadays, I stick to inside plumbing and running water when I need to cool off."

"It's deep enough for swimming in?"

"Not so much swimming, as lounging around while the water laps around you. On me, it wasn't waist deep. But it gets deep pretty quick if we get a gully washer. Been known to have a flash flood or two when she overflows her banks."

Ian laid down his cookie and looked at Miss Edna. "What's a gully washer?"

She chuckled and struggled to her feet. When he started to jump up, she waved him back and leaned forward on the kitchen table.

"A gully washer is what we old fogies call a quick, heavy thunderstorm, where the rain comes quick and hard. The ground gets wet so fast it can't absorb the water fast enough, and it causes flooding.

Ian committed the word and its meaning to memory, wanting to see if he could stump his dad with it later.

"Well, I got to get to the next batch of laundry. You need anything else?"

"No, ma'am. Thanks for the cookies."

She smiled at him, waving her hand around the kitchen.

"My pleasure, Ian. I used to love baking, but I don't get to do it so much anymore. Not as many folks stopping and staying here as there used to be."

Ian watched her walk out of the kitchen, her gait ambling and slow. He admired her because she still worked hard, and he figured it couldn't be easy. Judging from her appearance, she had to be ancient. Something outside the sunroom's window caught his eye, a movement that flickered in the corner of his vision, and he walked through the kitchen into the light-filled space.

A red bird perched on the edge of a bird feeder hanging from the eaves. A few more dark-colored ones swooped by, and the red bird let out a screech. Ian grinned, imaging she was warning the others to stay back and mind their own business until she was done. She wasn't gonna let them get close, not until she was good and ready.

Moving closer to the window, he studied the grounds behind the bed and breakfast. He'd never bothered before, because usually they only stayed overnight, except for recently when they'd spent the weekends looking for a place to live.

Several feet past the windows an area that had been cleared, then covered with small stones, mostly white but some tan colored. Shaped in a circular design, the center of the clearing held a firepit made of bigger stones of various sizes and colors. The center held a large metal container, bowl-shaped and rounded at the bottom, that was filled with pieces of wood.

Four wooden chairs with large backs encircled the firepit, painted forest green. Several feet away he spotted a fountain, the water bubbling up and spilling out of a large fish's mouth. Ian grinned and made fish lips, wiggling them several times.

He spotted a couple more areas that looked like large boxes made from wood, shaped like large rectangles. The wood looked old and gray, weathered with age, and worn smooth in places along the edges. Each of the two enclosed areas overflowed with all kinds of green, growing things. Most of them he didn't recognize, but from the orderly rows and abundant leaves, he'd guess it was Miss Edna's vegetable garden.

Beyond the firepit and fountain, a large forest spread out, huge pine trees stretching toward the sky. Lots of smaller trees and bushes grew in clusters lower to the ground, the earth covered with discarded pine needles, brown and brittle. Prickly pinecones lay scattered on the forest floor, like discarded soldiers from a long-forgotten battlefield.

Casting a glance over his shoulder, he didn't see anybody and moved closer to the door leading outside. He just wanted a closer look. Besides, he was tired of being trapped inside, with nothing to do. His video game was getting boring, and he'd have to talk to his dad about letting him use his allowance to get a new one.

After another surreptitious glance over his shoulder, he

opened the door and eased through, making sure it didn't make any noise as it closed. His first stop was the vegetable patch. Running his fingertips along the vibrant green, he grinned. When he spotted the carrot tops, he dipped his fingers into the dirt, exposing the brilliant orange color just beneath the surface. At least those he recognized.

He strolled over to the firepit area, and flopped down into one of the chairs, crossing his feet at the ankles. This was cool. Maybe if they were going to be here for a couple of days while they waited for the furniture, he could talk his dad into building a fire and they could get some marshmallows to roast. He'd never done them outdoors, only in the fireplace when he lived with…

Letting the thought trail off, he squeezed his eyes shut against the burning pain in his chest. No matter how many times his dad explained it wasn't his fault mom had left, he knew different. She'd been so unhappy, always crying when she didn't think he could hear. He'd tried not to do anything to upset her, but no matter what he did, nothing seemed to help. And she still left. Left him behind, tossed him aside like he was a snot-filled Kleenex.

Jerking his head up at the sound of a dog barking, his gaze searched the yard, but he didn't see anything. He loved dogs and really wanted one, but living in the condo, it wasn't fair to the animal to be cooped up. Something Ian understood well, because far too many days, that was exactly how he felt. Moving to Shiloh Springs wouldn't change that any;

he was simply exchanging one lonely location for another. Same problem, different location, that's all.

At another bark, he caught movement from the corner of his eye and spotted a dark brown dog. It stood just inside the tree line, and its coat looked like a melted chocolate bar. Cocking its head to the side, the dog studied him as closely as he studied it. From here, he couldn't tell if it was a male or a female, but despite the barking, he didn't think it was aggressive. In fact, from the rapidly wagging tail, it seemed friendly.

"Hey, pup. What are you up to?"

The dog took a tentative step forward at his voice, and then another, stopping to watch him with a guarded stare. Its pink tongue hung out of the side of its mouth and with a happy yip, the dog gave a playful lunge forward and then retreated, tail whirling a mile a minute.

Ian grinned at the dog's antics. Easing from the chair, he squatted down and patted his thigh, enticing the animal closer. After what seemed like forever, the dog took a tentative step forward, then another. Soon it stood within a foot of him. Reaching out his hand, palm down, Ian held his breath, hoping the dog would trust him because he really wanted to pet it.

A cold, wet nose pressed against his hand, the whiskers tickling against his palm. Ian ran his hand over the dog's head and scratched behind its ears. The dog responded by pushing his head into his hand, welcoming Ian's fingers digging into his coat, at least that's how it seemed to him.

This activity went on for several minutes as Ian played with the dog, laughing out loud when the dog flopped onto his back, wanting his belly rubbed. And it was definitely a male.

Inside the B&B a door slammed, startling the animal. Jerking beneath Ian's hand, the dog squirmed and wiggled free, heading for the trees. Without a single thought, Ian raced after the dog, disappearing into the dense foliage.

CHAPTER NINE

D errick reined in the urge to bang his head against the table in the conference room at the sheriff's office. This entire day had been one frustration after the next. The only bright spot had been closing on the new house. Everything since then had been downhill.

He hated leaving Ian alone at the B&B. It never would have happened if the situation Rafe had called about hadn't been serious. Ian didn't deserve to be treated like he was a secondary consideration, because he wasn't. If push came to shove, and he had to choose between his job and his son— his son came in first, every time.

"What's the hold-up? When you called, you said you had a handle on things."

Rafe ran a hand through his hair, his expression a mix of frustration and anger. He sympathized. Dealing with criminals and bad guys in the big city was a cakewalk compared to small-town life. Poor Rafe had to walk on eggshells, to keep the peace with the townsfolk, because everybody knew everybody, or was related to somebody. It probably felt like he was walking a tightrope without a safety net.

"There are days when I wonder why I thought being sheriff was a good idea. Today's one of them. Sorry I had to drag you away from your celebration."

Derrick leaned back in his chair and folded his hands across his stomach. "Not much of a celebration. The furniture isn't showing up for a couple of days. Ian and I are staying at the Creekside Inn with Miss Edna until the store can get it delivered." He shot Rafe a look. "My son is not a happy camper right now."

Rafe winced at his words. "Now I'm really sorry."

"We'll deal. What can you tell me about the situation? You said something about a missing person?"

"Yeah. Here's the thing. Eliza and Dennis Boatwright are unique characters here in Shiloh Springs. They both tend to overindulge a bit from time to time. Especially around the first of the month when their checks come in. Dennis also makes his own home brew."

When Rafe stopped talking and gave him a pointed look, Derrick realized the unspoken implication.

"Would I be erroneous in assuming Mr. Boatwright might also manufacture something a little stronger than beer?"

It wouldn't be unheard of, especially if they were older folks. Producing and selling moonshine was illegal, but more than a few people he knew still manufactured for their own personal use. On a scale of small potatoes versus more dangerous crimes, moonshine barely made a blip on the radar.

"I cannot confirm your hypothesis, but I won't deny it." Rafe grinned, his smile making him appear younger, more relaxed. "Anyway, Eliza's niece is visiting. Her baby sister's child. She's gotten to be more than her momma can handle, and she sent her to stay for a couple of weeks. We got a call from Eliza that Jennifer—the niece—hasn't been home in two days."

"Why'd she wait so long before calling?"

"She didn't come right out and say anything, but I got the impression this isn't the first time she's stayed out overnight. Jennifer has a cell phone, and we've tried calling. It goes straight to voice mail."

"Have you tried having the service provider check the GPS or ping the closest cell tower?"

Rafe shot him a *do-you-think-I'm-stupid* stare. "Chance is meeting with Judge Willis right now, getting the necessary warrants."

Derrick nodded, hating the red tape and hoops law enforcement had to jump through to get the job done. It was one of those necessary evils they all dealt with to protect the rights of the guilty and the not-so-guilty alike. Sometimes it felt like wading through quicksand to get the job done. But it was all worthwhile in the end when they were able to keep even one single person from harm.

"Does the aunt know if Jennifer has made any friends

since she's been here? Maybe she spent the night with a girlfriend and just didn't call."

"I've got Dusty getting as much pertinent information as he can, questioning neighbors and their kids. Since Jennifer's not enrolled in school here—yet—I doubt she's met many kids her own age."

"Does the aunt suspect somebody's snatched her?" Derrick drew in a deep breath, feeling a wave of anxiety flood him at how he'd feel if somebody took Ian. He'd search heaven and hell to get his son back, so he could sympathize with the Boatwrights.

"They don't really know what to think at this point. Jennifer's been petulant and mad because she was pretty much forced to leave home and come stay with family she barely knows. Eliza and her sister aren't especially close; there's a bit of an age difference between them. Her sister also didn't have Jennifer until she was older, so we're dealing with a teenager who probably thinks nobody understands her."

"All right, tell me how you want to handle this. It's your town, your team. I'm unofficial at this point because we don't know there's any reason to call in the FBI."

"I don't know. Something about this whole thing doesn't feel right. Either we're dealing with a pissed-off teen, who's angry at her family and has simply run off, which we can't rule out, or she's been snatched by a stranger. It hasn't happened in Shiloh Springs before, but anything's possible.

The closest we had was a little while back when Heath and Camilla were on the run. Thought somebody had followed them from Louisiana, but it turned out to be a couple who'd skipped town to be together. Borrowed a car, but the car's owner called it in as stolen."

Derrick chuckled. "I swear, Shiloh Springs has the most interesting cases for a small town. I rarely get these kinds of cases in Austin."

"Be thankful. People living in small towns know everything and everybody."

Derrick listened to Rafe's words and remembered something Antonio had mentioned in passing a few weeks prior. It wasn't any of his business, but again, since he was planning to be a part of this community, at least part-time, he might as well see what he could do to help.

"A little birdie told me you've had a bit of trouble with a petition circulating in town."

Rafe almost choked on the coffee he'd just drank, and he pounded his fist on his chest. "A little birdie? You mean my big mouth brother?"

"No comment."

Shaking his head, Rafe blew out an exasperated breath. "Yeah, someone's circulating a petition around the county, asking for me to be recalled from the position of sheriff, and for a special election to replace me."

"Are they crazy? You do an extraordinary job. Trust me, I've worked with lots of law enforcement, big and small town, and you're one of the finest. Your reputation is flawless. Trust me, I checked."

"Glad I passed scrutiny."

Derrick ignored the jibe and continued. "Any idea who or why they want you ousted?"

"Honestly? I've been too busy to deal with it. I was hoping if I ignored it, it would go away. Which backfired, because my folks found out, and Momma's going on the warpath. I pity whoever started the petition because she's out for blood."

"Good for her. I'll be happy to look into who's behind it, if you'd like. Since I'm now a proud homeowner within the city limits, I now have a dog in this hunt. I like knowing an honest man is looking out for the town's best interests."

A flush of red spread across Rafe's cheeks. "Appreciate it. I'm hopeful it won't be necessary. Chance's connections at the courthouse are going to do a little digging, see where it originated. We'll go from there."

Rafe's phone rang, and he answered it, giving Derrick a chance to check his. No missed calls from Ian. Kid hadn't texted, either. He shook his head, knowing he had a lot of ground to make up because he'd broken the trust with his kid by coming in to work. No matter how good his intentions, he felt guilty.

"That was Dusty. Jennifer's been hanging out with a group of teens who don't live too far from the Boatwrights. He's only been able to talk with one of them, but she thinks

Jennifer mentioned something about a boyfriend. He's going to check into it with the mother, see if there's anything there."

"It's a start. Okay, let's dig in and see if we can find Jennifer."

CHAPTER TEN

Daisy parked in front of the B&B, and slid from the driver's seat, reaching back into the car to grab a tote bag off the passenger seat. Ike had prepared a large takeout portion of pot roast to give to Miss Edna. He'd developed a soft spot for her elderly neighbor, and once or twice a week he fixed up a batch of leftovers for Daisy to drop off on her way home. It wasn't an inconvenience, since the B&B was close enough she could walk from her place to it.

Entering the front, she called out, "Miss Edna, it's Daisy."

Hearing a noise to her left, she glanced toward the office behind the front desk area, and spotted Miss Edna sitting behind her desk, a mound of paperwork sitting in front of her. The older woman's head hung down toward her chest and hearing a snuffling snore, Daisy knew she caught the other woman napping.

Not wanting to startle her, she walked into the kitchen and began unloading the food from the tote. Glancing at the amount Ike had sent, she couldn't help shaking her head. He'd sent enough food to feed several people, or for Miss

Edna to have leftovers for a few days.

Before she'd pulled the last container free, Miss Edna walked through the opening into the kitchen, yawning. Her eyes opened in surprise when she spotted Daisy.

"Afternoon, Miss Edna."

"Daisy gal, what are you doing?" She gestured toward the takeout packages stacked on the table.

"We featured pot roast today as the special, and Ike made a little too much. He thought you might like to have a meal you didn't have to cook and sent you some. I said I'd deliver it on my way home."

She watched Miss Edna draw in a deep breath, her eyes welling with unshed tears. More than once she'd dropped by with meals, and although Miss Edna always protested, she knew they were appreciated.

"I appreciate the thought, but I can cook."

"I know you can cook, but it's nice to have somebody else do all the heavy lifting once in a while. Now, all you have to do is heat it up when you're ready to eat."

"Well, at least let me—"

"Miss Edna, if you even reach for your wallet, I'm gonna walk right out that front door. You know I'm not going to take your money."

The older woman slid onto a chair and stared at the food like it was manna from heaven. It probably was for somebody who cooked breakfast and lunch for her guests, which the B&B provided for their paying guests. Not having to prepare, cook, and clean up after the dinner meal probably felt like winning the lottery.

"Thank you, Daisy, and tell Ike thanks, too."

"You're quite welcome."

At the sound of the sunroom door slamming, Daisy looked up to see Ian race into the kitchen. He skidded to a stop when he spotted her and Miss Edna, a guilty expression crossing his sweaty face.

"Oh, hi, Daisy."

"Ian. I thought you were hanging with your dad today."

Ian made a scoffing sound. "He had to work. The sheriff called him, and he ended up heading into town to do whatever he does."

Daisy might not know Ian all that well, but she could read enough between the lines to know he wasn't a happy camper. Whatever Derrick was working with Rafe on, it had better be pretty darned important to leave his son alone.

"Well, I'm heading home, where I'm going to make a big bowl of popcorn, put my feet up, and watch a movie. Feel like joining me, Ian? If your dad says it's okay, of course. I can give him a call and see if it's okay, that is, if you want to watch something."

Ian narrowed his eyes, contemplating her request. "What movie?"

She shrugged. "I've got Netflix, Hulu, and Prime. I figured I'd see what they've got and pick something. I'm in the mood for something with lots of guns and explosions. Action and adventure. Maybe something from Marvel."

At the look of relief in his eyes, she almost laughed out loud. Almost, because she knew he'd be embarrassed if she did. What did he think, that she'd force him to watch some chick flick? A romantic comedy with lots of kissing?

"Would you mind, Miss Edna, if I went with Daisy?"

Daisy was impressed at his show of manners in asking her permission. Most kids his age wouldn't think to ask. Now all she had to do was get his father to agree.

"As long as your father says it's okay, it's fine with me." She nodded at Daisy, and she felt warmth spread through her. It was nice to know she'd made the right choice, and Miss Edna's approval meant a lot.

Pulling out her cell phone, she dialed Derrick's number. It rang several times before he answered.

"Daisy? What's wrong?"

"Now why would you automatically assume something's wrong?"

"Maybe because you don't normally call me?"

She bit back a grin at his words, hearing the underlying teasing in his voice. "True. Nothing's wrong. I stopped by Miss Edna's to drop off some food and found out you're working with Rafe this afternoon. I wondered if you'd mind Ian coming to my place while you're working. I've got cable and streaming channels, and thought we could make a batch of popcorn and watch movies until you finish up at the sheriff's office."

"Daisy, you're a lifesaver. It would be great, if you don't mind. I know he's probably going stir crazy, but there's a situation I'm helping Rafe deal with, and—"

"I wouldn't offer if I didn't want to do it. Ian and I will have a junk food marathon to go with the movie. You're the one missing out because I happen to make great popcorn."

Derrick chuckled, and the deep rumbling sound did funny things to her insides. It made her feel all girly and giggly like a teenager. If she wasn't careful, she'd be mooning over a picture of him taped to the ceiling of her bedroom so she could stare at him every night.

Good grief, girl, get a grip.

"I'll call you as soon as I've got a handle on how long I'll be here. If the movie ends before I'm done, have Ian go back to the B&B and I'll see him when I get back."

"Sounds like a plan."

After hanging up, she gave Ian a thumb's up. At his answering grin, she knew she'd made the right decision. Plus, she'd get to spend a couple hours getting to know Derrick's son a little better.

"Miss Edna, if you need anything, you've got my number. Ian and I will be plopped in front of the TV, gorging ourselves on junk food."

"Y'all have fun. Thank you again for the pot roast. You're such a good girl."

Daisy almost snorted at being called a girl. She'd passed thirty years old a few years ago, and some days she felt twice that, especially after a particularly harrowing day at work.

Ian climbed in the front seat of the car, and they drove the short distance to Daisy's house. She grabbed the second package of food from the back seat, and they headed into the house.

"Uncle Joe, I'm home, and I brought company."

Her uncle wheeled down the hall into the living room, and she saw his eyes widen when he spotted Ian.

"Who's your young friend, Daisy?"

"Uncle Joe, this is Ian Williamson, Derrick's son. His dad's working this afternoon, so Ian and I are going to watch some movies." Holding up the tray of food, she added, "Brought you some pot roast."

"Excellent." He rubbed his hands together and wiggled his brows. "I'm starving."

"Surprise, surprise. You're always starving." She turned to Ian, "Let's go into the kitchen and we can see what snacks we've got. That'll give me time to heat this up for my uncle, and we can decide what we want to watch."

"Cool."

Uncle Joe wheeled himself into the kitchen, straight to the table. Daisy hoped he'd join them for the movie watching after he ate. She always felt guilty about leaving him here alone for a good chunk of the day, though she knew he understood, having run the diner for more years than she could count. His stroke had put an end to that, and other health issues caused added complications. For an active and outgoing man, she knew it had to be driving him crazy, being stuck in a wheelchair. Though friends stopped by often to visit, it wasn't the same as being in the heart of things.

"Let's see. Ian, how do you like your popcorn? Plain butter, or do you want everything but the kitchen sink?"

She watched his eyes light up as she took things from the overhead cabinet. Today, she felt like adding a whole host of goodies to the big bowl. She also took down an unopened package of double-stuffed Oreos. Doing a quick check of the freezer, she smiled at seeing several pints of ice cream on the shelf. It was her secret vice. Didn't matter what flavor, it was her kryptonite.

"I've never had kitchen sink popcorn. What's that?"

"Oh, Ian, you are in for a treat. Daisy makes the best kitchen sink popcorn." Uncle Joe raised a forkful of pot roast and popped it into his mouth, chewing.

"Kitchen sink popcorn means you throw in everything but the kitchen sink. First, you start with the popcorn. Then you add whatever sounds good. Today I've got chocolate-covered raisins. Salted cashews. Glazed pecans. Some caramel syrup. Hmm, what else do we have? Marshmallows, the tiny colored ones like you get in cereal. Don't tell anybody, but I order whole bags of them because I'm just a big kid who likes junk food. Can you think of anything else we can toss in there?"

Ian's eyes widened with each item she placed on the countertop. She watched as he fought a smile, and knew she'd got him. There wasn't a kid alive who didn't want to eat as much junk as their little heart desired. He deserved a little spoiling. Oh, it wasn't that she thought Derrick neglected him. Every word and action shouted how much he loved his son. But sometimes a child needed somebody else to treat them like they were special. Important.

"I can't think of anything you haven't said. Can I help?"

Grabbing two bags of microwave popcorn, she pointed to a cabinet. "Grab the big bowl from the middle shelf."

Within a few minutes, both bags had been popped, and Daisy dumped them onto a large baking sheet. On top of the popped kernels, she added all the things she'd mentioned to Ian, mixing them together, and pouring her kitchen sink special into the bowl.

"What would you like to drink? I'm going to have a Dr Pepper."

"Can I have the same?" Ian asked.

"Sure."

"Hand me one of those, too, Daisy." Uncle Joe looked up from his nearly cleared plate, and she handed him a cold bottle.

"Feel free to join us for the movie when you're done, Uncle."

"Can't. Chuck's coming by to pick me up. We're going to Willie's house to play cards."

Chuck was one of her uncle's best friends. He dropped by a couple times a week to visit, and a few months earlier, he'd finally convinced her uncle to get out of the house to visit his friends. Chuck owned a van, and he was strong enough to lift Joe in and out of the van. She was eternally grateful to Chuck because he gave her uncle a sense of independence he'd lost after he'd ended up in the wheelchair.

"Have a good time. Give me a call if anything comes up."

Handing the sodas to Ian, she picked up the giant bowl of popcorn and the bag of Oreos and headed for the living room. Sitting their haul on the coffee table, she picked up the remote and clicked on the TV.

"Let's see. Any idea what you want to watch?"

He shrugged. "Whatever you want."

"Come on, Ian. Isn't there something you've been wanting to see that you haven't had a chance to watch? Nothing R-rated, though. I don't want your dad arresting me."

Ian snorted a laugh, trying to smother the sound. "He wouldn't arrest you, Daisy. He likes you."

Butterflies fluttered in the pit of her stomach at his innocent words. Had Derrick talked to Ian about her? About his feelings? She quickly quashed down the emotions, doing her best to remember she couldn't afford to get involved with anybody—no matter how much she wanted to.

Deciding it was better to ignore his statement, she pulled up the menu of movies available. "Have you seen *Guardians of the Galaxy*?"

He nodded. "Yeah, I've seen it a couple of times. I haven't seen the second one, though."

"Well, let's see if they have it; yep, they do. Want to watch it?"

"Sure."

Ah, finally a little bit of enthusiasm. Looks like the way to Ian's heart is through his stomach with a side of Marvel movies.

"I love it. I've seen it a bunch of times. Here we go."

With the click of a button, she started the movie, watching the funny opening scene. She loved the soundtrack for the movie, the old classic songs recognizable, invoking a sense of nostalgia.

When Chuck knocked on the door, Uncle Joe simply waved a hand toward her and opened the front door, wheeling himself onto the porch. While the movie played, Ian lost himself in the film, and she lost herself in her daydreams about a certain tall, dark, and dangerous FBI agent.

CHAPTER ELEVEN

Derrick pulled up and parked in front of Daisy's house and cut the engine. Running a hand through his hair, he stared at the front door, wondering how he was going to explain to Ian that he had to go back to help with the missing girl. They'd spent hours looking for her, interviewing the family, and talking to the few friends Jennifer had in Shiloh Springs.

His gut told him she'd run off. Maybe alone or maybe with a guy. Her aunt and uncle seemed to be genuinely concerned, worried about her, and wanting her to come back. Her friends were hiding something. Whether they knew where she was or suspected something, they weren't saying. But the bottom line was a teenage girl was missing and needed to be found, hopefully safe and unharmed.

Climbing from the car, he crossed to the front porch and knocked softly on the front door. The porch light shone, illuminating the space. White wicker chairs stood side-by-side, with blue and white pillows on the seats. A small table painted a matching white sat between them, a flowering plant with red flowers blooming on top. He had no idea what it was. Gardening skills weren't high on his list of hobbies, but either Daisy or her uncle had a green thumb.

The front door opened quietly, and Daisy stood silhouetted in the golden glow from the porch light. The platinum blonde with the navy highlights framed her beautiful face, giving her an almost ethereal appearance. There was something about the woman that made his heart race every time he saw her, and now was no exception. He couldn't explain what it was about Daisy that made him think about things he hadn't considered in a long time. Why her? He'd seen women more beautiful than Daisy. Had even dated a few. Yet, whenever he was in her presence, and a lot of times when he wasn't, he couldn't think of anybody who sent his pulse pounding or made him contemplate things he'd sworn he'd never do again. Shaking his head, he pushed thoughts of the impossible from his mind. No, now wasn't the time to be thinking about whether he could seriously consider anything more than friendship. He had to think about making a home for his son. Ian had to come first and foremost. His son had never had the kind of home life he should, always coming in second place and Derrick was determined to change that.

"Hi, Derrick." Her voice held a husky quality, and his whole body stiffened at the sound. "Come on in."

He followed her into the house, his gaze taking in where she lived. The pale aqua walls and light hardwood floors gave her home a beachy feel, which somehow suited Daisy. He knew she shared the house with her uncle, but he didn't notice a lot of masculine touches. Bright prints decorated the walls, vivid sunsets, and tropical scenes, reinforcing the feeling of being on vacation. Definitely not something he'd expected to find in the center of small-town Texas.

Following in her wake, they ended in the kitchen. He'd spotted Ian on the sofa, his head resting on a pillow. A movie played quietly on the television, but his son slept through the explosions and fireworks rocketing across the screen.

"Looks like he's crashed. Hope he hasn't been too much trouble."

Daisy smiled. "We've had a blast. Ate tons of junk food, drank sodas, and watched Marvel movies. Fortunately, we bypassed the sugar rush and he fell into a food coma about twenty minutes ago. I'm not sure where he puts all that food, though. Must have a hollow leg."

"I'll take him off your hands and get him settled back at the B&B. I'm going to have to head back to the sheriff's office afterwards. We've got a missing kid, and the search is ongoing."

"That's awful. Can I ask who it is?"

Derrick ran a hand through his dark hair and rotated his neck, trying to work out the kinks before answering.

"A teenager named Jennifer Boatwright. She's the niece of a couple who live in Shiloh Springs."

"Oh, no! I know them. That's awful. Poor Eliza, she must be frantic."

"Rafe's got everybody on high alert, looking for her."

Daisy patted his forearm. "You must be exhausted. Have you eaten?" When he shook his head, she pointed to the chair beside the table. "Sit. You can take five minutes to eat. The least I can do is make you a sandwich."

He hadn't realized he was hungry until she mentioned food, and suddenly he was ravenous. He felt like Pavlov's dog, salivating at the thought of eating.

"If it's not too much trouble. Thank you."

"It won't take a minute. Roast beef okay?"

"Perfect."

He sat at the kitchen table and watched Daisy pull things from the refrigerator. Roast beef, lettuce, tomato, and spicy mustard. Reaching into an old-fashioned breadbox sitting on the counter, she pulled out a loaf of homemade bread and sliced two thick pieces. In less than two minutes, she laid a plate in front of him piled high with roast beef.

"This looks delicious."

"Eat, you must be starving. Oh, I've got soda, sweet tea, or water. What can I get you?"

"Water. I don't need any more caffeine right now. I'm already bouncing off the walls from all the coffee I've had." He sank his teeth into the sandwich and couldn't believe how good it tasted. This was great. He'd resigned himself to grabbing some fast food on the way back to the sheriff's office, but this beat a stale, overprocessed hamburger.

"You've all been working on this case all day?"

He nodded. "Pretty much."

"I should probably get some food together to take over. I bet everybody's starving." When she went to stand, he placed his hand over hers and she froze.

"Tessa and Beth brought food by. I slipped out to pick up Ian. Told them I'd be back in about an hour. I doubt they noticed, anyway. When I left, Rafe was face first in a bag of tacos."

Daisy grinned because she knew that look. Rafe did love Mexican food. He might singlehandedly be keeping Juanita's in business.

"You are a lifesaver, Daisy. I didn't realize how hungry I was. You are an amazing woman."

When she remained silent, he looked up from his plate and caught a look of surprise and something else cross her face. She quickly shut it down and pasted on a smile, but he'd noted it and wondered what he'd said that caused that expression. While he was generally good at reading people, some days Daisy was an enigma.

"I'm not. Sometimes I wish I could go back and change things."

"Like what?"

She braced her elbows on the table and rested her chin on her hands. "Being young and stupid. Making mistakes because I let my emotions overrule my sense."

There was an underlying emotion lacing her words. She'd never opened herself up like this before, and he wanted to know more. Know everything about her. Find out what made her tick, shaped, and molded her into the woman she'd become.

"We all make stupid mistakes when we're young, sweetheart."

He watched her body start at his words. What had he said wrong?

"You called me sweetheart."

I did, didn't I? And it feels right.

"Does that upset you?"

"Um, no?"

He chuckled at the questioning sound of her answer. "You don't sound very sure."

"It's just…I've never heard you use an endearment for anyone before."

He thought about that for a second, realizing it was true. "It feels right, Daisy. You're right, I don't usually show my feelings. I grew up in a household where we kept our emotions under rigid control. There weren't a lot of hugs and kisses. I knew my parents loved me, but they were not demonstrative people. I swore when I grew up, I'd be different. But it's a hard habit to break when it's all you've ever known."

"You seem to be doing a good job with Ian. He knows he's loved, and that's one of the most important things a child needs. You're making a home for him, both in Austin and here. Love him, be there for him, and it will all work out."

Without pausing to think it through, he picked up her hand and brought it to his lips, placing a kiss against the skin. Her indrawn breath revealed she'd felt something when his lips touched her, which was good because he'd felt something, too. Such a simple touch, yet it ricocheted deep within him, startling him, because it felt right.

"Daisy, I—"

"Don't." She got up and took several steps further into the kitchen. He stood, closing the distance between them, and rested his hands on her shoulders, leaning in close, whispering in her ear.

"Are you going to deny there's something between us? Because if you do, I'll call you a liar. You feel the same pull, the same attraction I feel for you."

She drew in a shaky breath and turned to face him. "I feel it too."

"Are you willing to do something about it? See where it leads? Because I am. I haven't felt like this in a long time. It's more than a simple attraction to a beautiful woman." Lifting his hand, he played with a lock of her hair, shifting his fingers through the navy blue highlights. "And you are a very beautiful woman, Daisy."

"Derrick—"

"Before you answer, I want to put all the cards on the table. It won't be easy, but then the best things never are. My job's in Austin. Yours in here, with your diner and your uncle. I would never ask you to give that up. Just like I can't toss my job aside and come to work in Shiloh Springs. And I'm a package deal. You get me, you also get my son."

A myriad of emotions crossed her face, and he read every one. The hesitation, the doubt, and the same yearning he felt. He knew they'd be good together, physically, emotionally, and everything in between. He also realized what he was asking wasn't fair. But he didn't care. Having Daisy in his life made him feel complete, and he didn't want to let go of that feeling.

The smile she gifted him shot straight to his soul. It was tender and sweet, and fully accepting of him, warts and all. She didn't know all the ugliness of his life, his job. Even his ex.

"I already love your son, Derrick. And I'm halfway in love with you. This is crazy. Insanity of the first order. Yet it's true."

Lifting his hands, he cupped her face gently, his thumbs gently caressing the softest skin he'd ever felt. Her eyes drifted closed, and he leaned close, focused on her lips. This would be their first kiss, and he wanted it to be unforgettable.

"Dad?"

Derrick jerked back at the sound of his son's voice. Ian stood barefoot in the doorway to the kitchen, rubbing his eyes. It was obvious he'd just awakened, hair standing on end and his T-shirt scrunched up on the bottom.

"Hey, bud. You were conked out when I got here."

"I guess I fell asleep watching Captain America."

"You ready to head back?"

"I guess." Ian faced Daisy, and a shy smile crossed his face. Taking a couple of steps into the kitchen, he walked up to her and gave her a big hug. "Thanks, Daisy. This was fun."

Daisy smoothed down his hair with a gentle hand, giving Ian a soft smile. "You are quite welcome. Any time you want to watch TV, just let me know."

"Go put your shoes on, kiddo. I need to talk to Daisy for a second, okay?"

Ian nodded and left the kitchen. Derrick pulled her close, liking the feel of her in his arms. "We're not finished, my sweet Daisy. We can make this work." Leaning forward, he dropped a quick kiss on the tip of her nose. "I'll call you tomorrow."

"Okay."

"I'm ready, Dad."

Derrick put an arm around Ian's shoulders and led him to the front door. Pulling it open, he paused for a second, turning to look at Daisy. She stood in the same spot, watching them both, an unguarded expression of such yearning on her face, he almost went back to her. He promised himself he'd find out what put that expression on her beautiful face. Whatever she wanted, whatever she needed, he'd find a way to make it happen.

"Goodnight, sweetheart."

She shook her head, obviously remembering their earlier conversation, but a tiny smirk quirked up her lips. With one last look, he pulled the door shut behind him, and drove to the B&B.

Now he had to face the wrath of one Ian Williamson when he told his son he had to go back to work. It wasn't going to be pretty.

CHAPTER TWELVE

Ian swiped and ended the phone call, feeling that now-familiar burning pain in the middle of his chest. It happened every time he talked to his dad recently. Guess today wasn't an exception. His dad hadn't made it back to the B&B the night before. Something about a girl who hadn't come home, and her family said she was missing. They hoped she was a runaway, but they still had to investigate because she wasn't old enough to leave.

He couldn't blame the girl if she had run away. More than once, he'd considered it himself. It wasn't that he didn't think his father loved him; he did. But he was an inconvenience. Living with his dad caused him trouble at work, because he had to make sure Ian always had someplace to be, somebody to watch him, so he could go to his job. And his dad's work was important—he caught the bad guys—which was a good thing.

Walking into the sunroom, he plopped down into one of the chairs, slouching down into its cushioned depths. Putting his phone on the arm of the chair, he stared out the window. It wasn't even noon and it was already hot. Unfortunately, he'd found out that was normal for Texas. Living in Louisiana with his mom, it got hot, but it felt different than here. Sometimes he wished he was back in Shreveport because they'd lived there longer than anyplace else.

Mom, why'd you leave me? I hate it here. Everything's different. Dad's cool, but he's never home, and when he is, he's always working. We haven't even moved into the new house, and where's Dad? At the sheriff's station instead of with me. I thought it would be different, moving to Shiloh Springs, but it's not. It's just a different place to sleep, but nothing else changed.

He lifted his head when he heard a snuffling sound. Glancing out the window, he spotted the dog he'd seen the day before. It was pawing around the firepit. No exactly digging, but making scratching-type movements at the rocks.

Standing from his slouched position, he opened the side door and walked outside. The dog froze when he spotted Ian, his nose in the air. Suddenly, his tail started wagging, a rapid staccato of motion.

"Hey, fella. You came back. Do you live around here?"

Ian cautiously moved closer until he stood a few feet away. Standing still, he waited. He knew enough about dogs to know he needed to be careful, let the dog come to him. One of the boys in his other school had gotten mauled by a dog, and Ian remembered the stitches all over the kid's arm and shoulder. He'd had to wear a sling for a long time while he healed.

After what seemed a long time, the dog moved forward

and sniffed Ian's hand, tail still wiggling his whole backside. When he stuck his nose against Ian's hand, he chuckled softly. Slowly squatting down, he wrapped an arm around the dog's neck, hugging him tightly, while the dog covered his face with kisses.

Suddenly, the dog wriggled away, giving a sharp, loud bark. Ian landed on his backside from the sudden movement, and the dog darted toward the tree line behind the B&B. Scrambling to his feet, Ian called out to the pup, who stopped right at the edge of the yard and turned to look at him. He gave another bark, as though demanding Ian come with him.

"Dog, I can't. I'm not allowed to leave the yard. Heck, I'm not even supposed to be out here. My dad would kill me if he knew."

The dog darted back toward Ian, stopping a few feet away. He gave a couple more barks and ran into the tree line. Ian moved closer, curious about what caused the dog to race away. Moving closer to the edge of the backyard, he peered between the canopy of trees, catching sight of the dog, who'd stopped and looked at him, as if encouraging him to follow him.

Ian felt a tugging in his chest, like a string connecting him to the dog. He wished the dog hadn't run off, because he wanted to play like they had the day before. Watching the black dog carefully, he cast a glance over his shoulder. He then straightened to his full height.

"Dad won't care. He's too busy thinking about everybody else. I'm not doing anything wrong. I just want to play with the dog."

A twinge of guilt shot through him as soon as the words left his mouth. He'd never deliberately disobeyed his dad. But he was tired. Tired of being last on his dad's list of priorities. Tired of being alone. He didn't have any real friends. When he'd been with his mom, they'd moved around all the time. Every year, a new school in a new place. Always the new kid in school.

Straightening to his full height, he took a tentative step toward the dog, and then another. The dog gave a happy yip and darted farther into the woods. After one more glance over his shoulder, Ian walked into the woods.

Derrick squeezed the bridge of his nose between his thumb and forefinger, wondering if this day would ever end. He'd spent most of yesterday and all of today either at the sheriff's office or out in the field, looking for the missing Jennifer. Except for the short time he'd taken off to pick up his son from Daisy's, he'd been working.

Guilt rocketed through him at the thought of Ian. What a mess. Here he'd picked up and gotten the second home in Shiloh Springs so he could spend time with his son, away from the job. They hadn't even moved into the house yet and where was he? Up to his eyeballs with a case.

Daisy's unspoken disapproval had stung. Not that he blamed her. She understood he couldn't just turn off his need to help people. It was as ingrained in him as breathing. No, her disapproval hadn't been personal, she hurt for his son. When he'd gone to pick up Ian and take him back to the B&B, he'd been asleep on her sofa, with a movie playing softly in the background. Daisy had taken pity on him and fed him. He knew that was a part of her, the nurturing soul she possessed. It made her a kind, loving person, and also the perfect choice to run the town's diner. She cared about the town's residents and showed that by feeding them and giving them a refuge from life's struggles.

Glancing at the phone in his hand, he winced at the time. It was almost midafternoon. So far, there hadn't been any sign of Jennifer. He still felt one of her acquaintances knew where she was because according to her aunt and uncle, she didn't have any money. Didn't have a car. Plus, she didn't know that many people in Shiloh Springs. Two and two didn't add up to four in this case.

He should call Ian. Check on him. Maybe—

"Hey, Derrick!" He heard Rafe's voice call down the hall, and he sprang to his feet, meeting the man as he strode from the front of the office. "We've got a lead."

"About bloody time," he muttered.

"Eliza called her sister, pumping her for information. Jennifer's mother finally admitted Jennifer has a boyfriend

KATHY IVAN

back home that her mother disapproves of and wanted them apart. He's older than her, and a bad influence. Keeps her out all night, and Mom's sure he's giving her drugs. The boyfriend showed up at her mother's house three days ago, demanding to know where Jennifer was, and she told him to take a hike. Jennifer was out of his reach, and she planned to keep it that way. That same night, when Jennifer's mother went to work, her place was broken into and ransacked. Might have been a coincidence, but seems a little too convenient if you ask me."

"You think Jennifer's boyfriend found something to indicate she was in Shiloh Springs and showed up here?"

"It tracks."

Derrick rolled the scenario around in his head. Yeah, he could see some love-smitten teenager making his way to Shiloh Springs looking for his girlfriend.

"Anybody checked to see if the boyfriend is still in Jennifer's hometown?"

"Waiting to hear back from the local police force. What do you wanna bet he's skipped town and picked up Jennifer?"

"You think they've gone out of state?"

Rafe shook his head. "I hope not, because then you'll definitely be here on official business. Jennifer is underage, and her boyfriend is twenty-two. The family would probably want him charged for kidnapping and transporting across state lines."

116

Derrick's head dropped to his chest. "This mess just keeps getting better and better." Picking up his phone, he stood. "I need to check in with Ian. He's mad because I promised I wouldn't work while we were here getting settled into the new place. I broke that promise. He hasn't said anything, but I know he's upset."

"Dude, I'm sorry. Do you need to go be with him? I can call you—"

"I should stay, at least until you hear back from the boyfriend's local cops. Let me call him, touch base. I have the feeling I'll have a lot of groveling to do when this is over."

Walking out into the hall, Derrick hit the speed dial for his son's phone, listening to it ring. And ring. When it went to voicemail, he left a short message and disconnected. He'd give it another ten minutes and then call back. Next time, Ian better answer.

Stretching, he continued walking until he stood outside the sheriff's office. He was tired, weary to his bones. The job in Austin kept him running twenty-four seven recently. Sometimes he wondered if there was anybody in the state who wasn't doing something illegal.

He glanced up and down Main Street, taking in the quaint, homey feel of the small town. There was something about the place that sank into his soul, making him feel grounded in a way he hadn't in a long time. This was what he wanted to share with his son. Ian had been shifted around his whole life. His mother hadn't provided the most stable home life, moving from city to city, and Derrick felt guilty enough over the divorce he hadn't caused a stink when she hauled their son along with her. He'd gone along with their lawyers' suggestion for her to have primary custody, since his job entailed a higher degree of danger, and often kept him out of town for days or weeks at a time. It would have been unfair to Ian for him to constantly be shifted from Derrick's place to his mother's, and back again. Liberal visitation rights had been negotiated, but it wasn't the same as having his son with him every day. He'd failed his son on so many levels, and it looked like nothing had changed.

"Williamson, good to see you."

Derrick started at the voice, recognizing Douglas Boudreau. The older Boudreau was the patriarch of the Boudreau clan, and from everything he'd heard and seen about the older man, his sons pretty much worshipped the ground he walked on.

"Douglas. How've you been?"

"Can't complain. Business is skyrocketing with all the new builds. People all wanting new construction these days instead of renovating existing buildings. Of course, that makes the wife happy, because it's more properties to list."

"I talked to Ms. Patti yesterday—or it might have been the day before. We closed on the new house."

Douglas nodded, and Derrick was sure his wife had filled him in on all the details. One thing he'd learned with dealing with the Boudreaus: Ms. Patti had her finger on the pulse of everything that happened in Shiloh Springs. There wasn't much that got past her, and she most likely kept her husband in the loop.

"How's Ian dealing with settling in?"

Derrick drew in a deep breath before answering. "We haven't moved in yet. There's a delay in getting the furniture we ordered delivered. We're staying at the B&B for the next day or so, and then I'll have to head back to Austin. I'd hoped we'd get things settled, so the next time we came to Shiloh Springs, it would be for an honest-to-goodness vacation."

"Let me talk to the missus. She'll get things straightened out in no time." Douglas clamped his hand on Derrick's shoulder, his grip solid and brooking no argument. "You here helping Rafe with this missing person case?"

"Yes. Been here pretty much all night. Came out to call and check on Ian. I hated leaving him alone at the B&B. He's not happy I'm working. I promised I wouldn't since we were getting settled in the new house. I have the feeling I'm in the doghouse as far as my son's concerned."

Douglas didn't speak for the longest time, long enough he wondered if their conversation was finished. He'd had dealings with the Boudreaus for a year now, ever since Antonio had started working at the FBI Austin office. They'd dealt with several overlapping cases, in addition to developing a friendship with all the Boudreaus. Through that time, he'd learned that Douglas was a man of few words.

Stoic and solid as the Rock of Gibraltar, the man dispensed a wealth of knowledge few could match. An understanding of right and wrong that went bone deep, Derrick would want Douglas at his side in a firefight every time.

"Keeping our word is tantamount, especially with our children. There are times when life collides with our desires. Especially when the welfare and possibly a life is on the line, like with this missing person case. Ian's a good lad, he'll understand and forgive you. Might not be immediate, because boys, especially preteen ones, can hold onto a grudge like you wouldn't believe." Douglas chuckled, then added, "Antonio is a perfect example. That boy was like a bulldog with a rope. He could hold onto the smallest slight for hours, sometimes days. But he was a thinker, and he'd look at every side, every angle, every excuse, and weigh each. He'd finally come around, accept the apology of whoever offended him, and then it was forgotten like it never happened."

"Ian's a good kid, but he's still adjusting to living with me full time. His entire life's been disrupted, with his mother heading for parts unknown. She's only called once since she left. I hope eventually she'll get her head screwed on straight, but in the meantime, he's dealing with a new home, a new school, and trying to come to terms with a father who's in his life twenty-four seven. It's a lot for a nine-year-old to have to deal with."

Douglas nodded and pointed toward the phone still in Derrick's hand. "Give him a call. See if he wants to spend the day at the ranch. I can have Dane pick him up. My wife's sticking close to the Big House today, rallying the troops. Making sure the Boatwrights have everything they need, and that somebody's there with them until the girl's found."

"Thanks, Douglas. I'll ask him. At least at the ranch, he'd have things to keep him occupied other than video games. I swear, between the ones on his phone and the ones on his Nintendo, I rarely see his face."

Douglas' chuckle clearly showed he understood where Derrick was coming from. Then again, he'd raised eleven boys, so he probably did.

"Well, just let me know, and I'll make the arrangements. Now, I'm going to head in and talk to Rafe. Figured if he's going to set up a search party, I'd volunteer able bodies from the construction crews."

"That's a great idea. He's got Dusty, Jeb, and some locals already checking sites, but we might have to extend this into a larger search."

"Let me talk to him; you talk to your son."

Douglas turned and walked into the sheriff's office, and Derrick heard Sally Anne greet him warmly. This was another thing he liked about Shiloh Springs. People were genuinely friends, generous souls, who'd go out of their way to help. While there were good people in the big city, there wasn't the sense of connection he felt here. If his job didn't keep him in Austin, he'd probably move here full time. Unfortunately, chances of that were slim to none.

Taking a deep breath, he hit dial and waited.

CHAPTER THIRTEEN

D aisy grabbed the cardboard box and began loading takeout boxes inside. Things had slowed down after the morning breakfast rush, and she'd asked Ike to make up some hot meals for the folks down at the sheriff's office. She'd talked to Dusty when he'd stopped by hours ago, and he'd mentioned Rafe and Derrick had worked through the night, coordinating and overseeing the search for the Boatwrights' missing niece.

Piling containers filled with scrambled eggs, sausage, bacon, a tray full of biscuits, and a big leakproof container of sausage gravy into the box, she added plates, napkins, and silverware. A couple of cartons of orange juice and apple juice joined the mix.

She glanced around the kitchen, looking to see if she'd forgotten anything. It might not be much, but making sure the people looking for Jennifer had a hot meal in their bellies made her feel like she was at least doing her part.

Hefting the large box in her harms, she walked out of the kitchen and ran smack into Derrick. She gave a little oomph sound, juggling her precarious load, and he quickly lifted it from her arms.

"Thanks."

"No problem. Where do you need this?"

She smiled ruefully. "Actually, that food is headed your way. I thought y'all might like a hot meal after working all night."

"That's very thoughtful. I'm sure they'll appreciate it." He placed the box on the counter and turned back toward Daisy. "I wanted to thank you again for looking after Ian."

"It wasn't a problem. I didn't have any plans, and Uncle Joe wasn't going to be home. I'd probably have vegged in front of the TV anyway, so why not have company?"

At his long, slow smile, the butterflies in her stomach started doing the cha-cha, and she placed her hand against it, trying to quell the riotous feeling coursing through her. It wasn't fair. He had the sexiest smile she'd ever seen, and when he turned it on her, she wanted to melt into a big puddle. But not here. Not now. This was her place of business. She needed to remain cool, calm, and collected, not act like a besotted teenager with her first crush.

"I'm sure he'll thank you. He fell asleep the minute his head hit the pillow, out like a light." He drew in a deep breath, and she watched his shoulders and chest move with the action. Her fingers itched to explore all the muscles beneath his button-front shirt.

"I didn't mind. What's he doing today, while you're here—I mean at the sheriff's station—not *here* here."

"Probably glued to one of his video games. I've been trying to call and he's not answering, which is a huge problem I'll be addressing with him when I get back to the B&B. It's one of our no-exception rules. He always answers when I call. But he's pissed at me right now. Probably sulking in our room."

"I'm here for several more hours, but I can drop in a check on him when I leave if you'd like."

"That's not necessary. I'm trying to get hold of Ian because Douglas Boudreau thinks he should go out to the ranch this afternoon. Probably wouldn't hurt Ian to be around the animals, plus Ms. Patti and Dane will be there, so he won't be alone. Except he's not answering his phone. If I can't get hold of him, I'll have to go and check on him."

"Derrick, you've got enough on your plate right now. And it's on my way home, so it's not like I'm going out of my way. Tell you what, if you hear from him in the next couple hours, call me. Otherwise, I'm going to worry. Besides, I have to drop off food for Miss Edna."

Derrick's hand raised to cup her cheek, and Daisy closed her eyes, soaking in the feel of his slightly callused hands against her face. It had been a long time since anybody had touched her with tenderness, and she wanted to remember this moment. It probably didn't mean anything to him, but to her it was everything.

"You are a special woman, Daisy Parker. I don't think I've ever met anybody with a heart as big as yours."

"I—you'd better get this stuff to the sheriff's office, or it's going to get cold. Tell Rafe I'll pick up the dishes and stuff later."

"See you soon, Daisy."

Derrick lifted the heavy box like it weighed nothing and headed for the front door. If only he realized he carried far more than food with him. He carried her heart. And didn't that thought scare her half to death?

Ian trailed behind the black dog, following as he darted and weaved through the tall trees. It was darker here, the branches over his head filled with bright green leaves and thick limbs. He didn't want to get too far away from the B&B or get lost. A tinge of anger speared him when he thought about how mad his dad would get because Ian disobeyed the rules.

You know what? I don't care. He doesn't care anyway, or he wouldn't have gone to work. He doesn't even want to be with me anyway. I'm not doing anything wrong. I'm not.

The dog suddenly raced ahead, almost a blur of motion, and Ian stumbled over a large branch, falling to his knees. He grimaced when stood, and noticed a muddy patch on the knee, along with a jagged tear in the denim.

"Dang it. Dad's gonna kill me."

A sharp yip sounded ahead of him, and he gamboled

toward the sound, gangly legs racing to catch up. Everything around him was different than anything he'd ever seen. The closest he'd ever gotten to real woods had been on television. He was a city kid, and Shiloh Springs seemed like a whole different world to what he was used to.

"Come on, dog. Where are you?"

He glanced to the left and right, not spotting the blur of blackness he'd been following. Slowly spinning in a circle, he scanned his surroundings again, a tingle of fear racing down his spine.

"Dog?"

The only sound greeting him was silence. Shoot, he'd been stupid, he realized. He'd gone farther than he'd thought. There was no path leading him back to the B&B.

Think. It can't be that far, right? You can do this, find your way back.

His heart beat within his chest so hard it almost hurt, and he swallowed past the giant lump in his throat. Everything looked the same. All the trees loomed over him like giants, branches reaching toward him like arms, ready to snatch him away.

The stupid dog was nowhere to be seen. Oh, man, he wished he'd never followed him. This was all his fault. Well, mostly, because Ian admitted he was partially to blame because he'd followed along behind the dog like a dummy.

The sounds around him sounded like somebody had turned the radio up too high. Loud and, if he was honest, scary. Drawing in a shaky breath, he took several steps forward, figuring he'd eventually come out of the woods, either back at the B&B or maybe onto a road. Might run into the creek Miss Edna talked about, and he could follow it until he found somebody.

A loud crack off to the side sounded like a gunshot, and forgetting everything he'd just decided, Ian took off running, dodging around trees and fallen branches, racing forward. All he could think about was getting away from whatever made the noises.

He ran until he got a stitch in his side, finally slowing from the pain. His breaths dragged through his lungs, panting through his mouth to breathe. Finally stopping, he sucked in air, bent over at the waist. After catching his breath, he straightened, listening to the sounds around him. The birds chirped, a sound he was familiar with.

That's not scary. Birds won't hurt me.

Taking a tentative step forward, he glanced toward the ground and froze. Just feet from him, almost invisible against the leaves and dirt on the forest floor, he saw movement. It almost looked like a shadow at first, but his gut knew different.

All the spit in his mouth dried up, and he swayed where he stood. A snake? It was the first one he'd ever seen in real life. Seeing them in the zoo didn't count, because they were behind big, thick glass and couldn't hurt him. But this one wasn't behind glass. It wasn't a picture in a book. It was real and it was moving—and it was coming at him!

Ian turned and ran, not sure where he was going, only that he needed to get away from the snake. He hadn't heard any rattling noise. Those were poisonous, he knew, but he wasn't sticking around to try and see if there were any beads on its tail.

Never stopping to look back, he ran. Ran until his legs felt like they would collapse beneath him, but he didn't stop. He couldn't stop. One thing was certain. He hated the woods. He hated Shiloh Springs. And he wanted to go home.

Plunging forward, tears ran down his face, and he wiped at them. Inside, fear ruled everything, overriding everything. All he could think about was finding his dad. He'd take him back to Austin, and they'd never have to come back to Shiloh Springs again.

A sob caught in his throat when his foot tangled on a large root sticking out of the ground. He sprawled face-first onto the ground, and a primal scream broke free. The urge to curl up into a ball and rock back and forth was strong, but if he stayed on the ground, Ian knew something even worse than a snake would get him. He'd watched enough nature shows on TV, there were dangerous animals who could maul him, tear him to bits.

He grabbed onto the tree closest to him and pulled himself up. Everything sounded eerily quiet, not even a breeze rustling the leaves. And it seemed darker. Why was it getting dark? It wasn't late enough to be getting dark.

Ian bit back a sob and scrubbed away his tears. He wanted his dad to come and find him. He was dirty and scared and he wanted to go home right now.

I'll call him. He'll come and get me. I don't like it here anymore.

Reaching into his pocket, he patted it. It was empty. Nearly frantic, he dug through all his pockets before remembering he'd set down his phone in the sunroom before he'd spotted the dog.

Oh, man, he was in so much trouble. It was the one rule his dad insisted on—always have his phone. Hanging his head, he almost gave in to the urge to cry. He was such a screwup. Nothing but a waste of space. Mom had left him behind. He was nothing but a responsibility to his dad. Now he'd messed up and done not one, but two, of the things his dad told him not to do. Not to leave the B&B and to always have his phone.

A roll of thunder rumbled in the distance, the ground vibrating beneath his feet. Ian felt a drop of water ping against his face and looked up. The sky had darkened more, and he realized what he saw between the branches overhead were fat, dark clouds.

Great, just what I need. Stuck in the woods with a disappearing dog, a snake, and now rain. Can this day get any worse?

CHAPTER FOURTEEN

D errick carried the box of food into the conference room at the sheriff's office. While they dug in, he stepped out of the room. Irritation had him ready to drive straight to the bed and breakfast and have it out with his son for his disobedience. Ian knew better than to ignore him, not answer the phone when he called.

Instead, he did the next best thing. Grabbing his phone, he dialed.

"Creekside Inn." Miss Edna's deep gravel came through loud and clear. She had one of the deepest voices Derrick ever heard from a female.

"Miss Edna, it's Derrick Williamson. Sorry to bother you. Have you seen my son?"

"Ian? Saw him a little bit ago. He's fine. He was playing video games in the sunroom last time I saw him."

Derrick blew out the breath he'd been holding. All that worrying for nothing. Guess Ian was pitching a fit and giving him the silent treatment. Hopefully, he would be over his snit by the time he got back to the B&B.

"Thank you, Miss Edna. He wasn't answering my calls,

and I thought I'd better check on him."

"Boys need their independence. Growing pains and all. Don't you worry, if there's anything to worry about, I'll give you a call."

"Appreciate it. I'll drop by later and talk with him."

After disconnecting the call, Derrick slid the phone in his back pocket and leaned back, scrubbing his hands across his face. It was tempting to bang his head against the wall, vent his frustration with the last two days. First the furniture delay, then dealing with Ian's petulant attitude, then the missing girl's case. He was supposed to have a long weekend off, doing nothing more intense than picking where the new furniture would go.

"Did you ask Ian about going to the Big House?"

He turned at Douglas' voice and shook his head. "He's not answering my calls."

Douglas chuckled and leaned against the wall directly across from Derrick. "Fortunately, I didn't have to deal with that when my boys were young. They weren't allowed to have cell phones. Not until they were in high school. If they wanted to avoid talking to me, it meant heading in the other direction when they spotted me."

"At least I know Ian's alright. I called Miss Edna over at the B&B, and she told me he's sitting in the sunroom playing games on his phone."

"I can drop by and talk to him."

"Appreciate the offer, Douglas, but he's fine where he is."

Douglas pushed himself off the wall and straightened. "I'm heading back to the site to coordinate with Liam. We'll line up volunteers for searching around the Boatwright property." He tapped the rolled-up paper in his hand. "I've got detailed maps and we'll start doing a grid search. If she's anywhere around there, we'll find her."

"Appreciate your help. I'm more used to dealing with searches in more heavily populated areas, with a lot more buildings to hide in."

"And isn't it a shame we have to know how to do something like this?"

"Yeah."

"Well, I'd better get going. Search is gonna be harder since there's a storm moving in." Douglas saluted him with the sheaf of papers and headed toward the front, and Derrick went back into the conference room. Dusty, Sally Anne, and a couple of the volunteers who'd been helping out were finishing their meals and cleaning up the table before heading back to their jobs.

"Derrick, I just heard from the local police. Jennifer's boyfriend hasn't been located anywhere in their town."

"He's here—or at least he was." Derrick was certain of it.

"That's what my gut's telling me."

Sally Anne stuck her head around the corner of the door. "Sheriff, somebody's here to see you."

"Unless it's an emergency, tell them to come back."

"Oh, trust me, I think you'll want to talk to her."

Rafe looked at Derrick, who shrugged, and waved to-ward the door in an *after you* motion. Standing just inside the front door stood a middle-aged woman and a young girl, probably mid-to-late teens. His gut told him something big was about to happen. It was that familiar instinct, the one that tingled when he was getting the final piece to a puzzle.

"Mrs. Dobbins, Pamela, what can I do for you?"

"Sheriff, my daughter has something to tell you."

Rafe shifted his attention to the daughter, and Derrick's body stiffened, anticipation and a sense of foreboding edging closer. He had a good idea of what the teen was about to say, hoping he was right.

"Pamela, what's going on?"

Pamela's big blue eyes filled with tears, and she brought her hands up, covering her face. "I'm sorry, I'm so sorry. I promised not to tell anybody, but then everybody started searching for her, and she made me swear, and—"

"Pamela, take it slow. Who made you swear not to tell?"

She looked up, sniffling. Tears stained her cheeks, and her nose had started running from crying, her face blotchy. "Jennifer."

Rafe shot him a glance.

"Jennifer Boatwright?" At Pamela's nod, he continued. "What did you promise her?"

"She was *really* upset about her mom sending her to Shiloh Springs. Her mom is a real…not a nice person. Won't let Jennifer see her boyfriend, doesn't want her to spend time with her friends. Jennifer said it was like living in a prison camp."

"Tell him the rest," her mother demanded. "Pamela befriended the girl. Jennifer's been hanging around our house, at least until the last couple of days. I haven't seen hide nor hair of her, but she has." She jerked a thumb toward her daughter.

"Mom!"

"Ladies, let's take this slow. Pamela, we know Jennifer was unhappy about having to stay with her aunt and uncle. We also know her boyfriend is here. Is she with him?"

Pamela's eyes seemed to get even bigger, and Derrick held onto what little patience he had. Prying answers out of reluctant witnesses had never been his strong suit, so he was glad Rafe had to do the talking. He was impressed at how he treated both women with kid gloves, not showing any emotion. He wished they'd get to the point though, because he wanted the missing girl found, the case closed, so he could get back to Ian.

Pamela swallowed nervously a couple of times before answering in an almost whisper. "Yes."

Rafe reached forward and took both of her hands in his. "Where are they? I need to talk to her, make sure she's okay."

"I don't know."

Her mother rolled her eyes and made a scoffing sound. "She's lying. I caught her on the phone talking to Jennifer this morning." She spun toward her daughter. "You tell the sheriff where Jennifer is right now. Her family is scared to death with worry. They deserve to know she's okay. Would you want me to worry about you if you disappeared, not knowing if you were hurt, or kidnapped, or dead? You know her family, do they deserve to suffer like that?"

"No, ma'am." Her gazed darted to him, as if she'd just realized somebody else was standing there. "Who's he?"

Without even glancing in his direction, Rafe answered. "Derrick Williamson, special agent with the FBI."

Pamela's mouth dropped open at the word FBI. Derrick almost laughed, realizing Rafe was using him as the boogey-man. Most people never had to deal with the Feds ever in their lives, and they had a reputation for being bad to the bone. He didn't mind being the bad guy if they got the answers needed to find Jennifer.

"FBI? Somebody called the FBI?"

Rafe gave a long-suffering sigh. He was probably as tired as Derrick. They'd both been going for over twenty-four hours with no sleep, with the day filled with stress, worry, and uncertainty, along with dealing with the distraught family.

"Jennifer has been missing for more than twenty-four hours. Since we didn't have evidence she was a runaway, we had to assume somebody kidnapped her."

Pamela twisted her hands together, wringing them over and over. "Kidnapped? Oh, no. This is getting worse and worse. Sheriff, Jennifer wasn't kidnapped. She's eloping."

"Pamela, Jennifer isn't old enough to get married legally. She would have to have written permission from her parents to get married, and her mother hasn't given her consent."

"Um, she—I mean Jennifer—forged her mom's signature. She didn't think she'd get caught, at least not until it was too late."

"Pamela, do you know where they are? I need to find her, talk to her. She could be in a lot of trouble, and I want to help her."

Pamela sniffled again. "They..." Her voice trailed off with a sob. Derrick knew they needed to treat her gently. She was little more than a kid herself. Probably thought it was cool and exciting to help her friend be with the man she loved. A modern-day Romeo and Juliet. He shook his head. Ah, the folly of youth. Time for him to step in. He cleared his throat and at Rafe's nod, he was on.

"Pamela, I want to know where Jennifer Boatwright is, and you're going to tell me. Sheriff Boudreau might be willing to treat you with kid gloves, but believe me, I have no problem arresting you for obstruction of justice. It's a serious offense and carries a large fine and possible jail time. You seem like a nice young lady and a loyal friend, but I don't think Jennifer would want you to go to prison, do you?"

"Prison?" Her mother's high-pitched squeal could probably be heard all the way to the town line. Derrick ignored her, while Rafe talked with her softly.

"They're in Santa Lucia, at a motel. I was supposed to

bring them money, and then they're going to Oklahoma to get married."

The words spewed from Pamela's lips, fast enough he almost didn't understand her. But he knew where Santa Lucia was, in the next county over from Shiloh Springs. If they left now, they could make it there in less than an hour.

"Pamela, I need the name of the hotel, and the name they are registered under."

She gave him the information, her whole body trembling. He winced, hating that he'd scared the child because she was still one. It was like hitting a puppy with a stick, looking at her shaking, waiting for the next swing.

"Thank you, Pamela."

"Mrs. Dobbins," Rafe turned to the mother, "I'm going to have Dusty take a statement from you and Pamela. Thank you for stepping forward and telling the truth."

Derrick watched Rafe lead the two back to his office, getting Dusty from the conference room. A couple minutes later he was back, cowboy hat in hand.

"You planning to go with me?"

"Yes. Hopefully, it won't be necessary, but you need backup. I'm game."

Climbing into Rafe's car, they headed for Santa Lucia. Pulling out his phone, he texted Ian, leaving him a message that he'd be back soon. He frowned when Ian didn't respond.

Guess I've got a few more fences to mend when I return.

CHAPTER FIFTEEN

Daisy double-checked to make sure the back door of the diner was locked. Today was her day to close and lock up, and then she'd head home. They closed early on Sunday afternoons, and she was more than ready to relax and put her feet up.

Her brow furrowed when she realized she hadn't heard from Derrick if Ian had gone to the Big House for the afternoon. This missing girl case had everybody on edge, and she knew search parties were out in several areas of Shiloh Springs. Ms. Patti had called her earlier, asking if she'd provide food tomorrow in case they needed to do official organized searches. She'd gladly volunteered. Being a part of the community, pitching in when there was a need, made her feel like she belonged.

Turning off the lights, and locking the front door, she took a deep breath, standing for a moment in front of the big picture window of her diner. Her diner, her sanctuary from the past. She'd made a lot of mistakes before coming to Shiloh Springs. Things that most people in town didn't know and she hoped they never found out.

Climbing behind the wheel of her car, she drove toward home almost on autopilot. Turning onto her street, she jumped when her phone rang, and she slid her hand into the pocket of her purse where she always kept it.

"Hello."

"Daisy. Thank goodness you answered."

The panic in Miss Edna's voice had her hands tightening on the steering wheel. Something was wrong and it had her elderly neighbor in a tizzy.

"Miss Edna, are you okay? What's wrong?"

"It's not me. It's Ian."

Ian?

"What about him?"

"He's missing. I've looked everywhere and I can't find him."

"I'm almost there. Hang on for another couple of minutes. We'll find him."

"Bless you. I'm scared to death. I don't know where he might be."

"I'm sure he's around. Don't worry. I'm pulling up in front right now. I'll be right in."

She disconnected the call, slammed the car into park, and yanked the keys from the ignition. Racing inside, she found Miss Edna standing in the middle of the B&B's lobby, wringing her hands and looking around frantically, like she was lost and didn't know which way to turn.

"I'm here. Let's sit down and you can tell me what's

going on."

"We don't have time to sit, child. Ian's missing."

Taking Miss Enda gently by the arm, she led her over to the overstuffed chair in the lobby and eased her into it. "Taking two minutes to sort things out won't hurt anything, and it'll give me a better idea of where to look. Take a deep breath and tell me what happened."

"I was supposed to watch him. I told his father everything was fine. But it's not. I fixed lunch, then went about doing the chores. It took me a little longer because I didn't sleep well and was moving a little slow. I...I didn't even notice Ian hadn't eaten his lunch until a while ago. Daisy, I've looked everywhere. I even climbed up to the attic, thinking maybe he'd gone exploring. He isn't here."

Daisy's mind was racing, going over all the places a young boy might disappear to at the B&B. The old Victorian was huge, with several bedrooms. Lots of places a curious kid could find himself lost in.

"Alright, Miss Edna. Here's what we're going to do. I want you to stay right here in the lobby, while I do a quick look for Ian." When she started to protest, Daisy continued, "You can see almost all of the first floor from here. You can shout if you see him. I'll be right back."

Before Miss Edna could say another word, Daisy sprinted up the steps leading to the second floor. She called out his name as she went, exploring all the nooks and crannies, and opening each door. Nothing. Ian wasn't hiding out. He hadn't fallen asleep somewhere or lost track of the time.

Ian wasn't anywhere in the B&B.

Climbing down the stairs, she moved into the kitchen, seeing the plate of food on the table. It hadn't been touched. Opening the door to the pantry, she glanced inside, knowing before she did it was fruitless, but she had to check anyway.

Looking through the opening between the kitchen and the sunroom, she noted the big black clouds covering most of the sky. It had drizzled and sprinkled on and off for the last couple of hours, but she knew it wouldn't be long before the rain burst free in earnest.

Walking into the sunroom, she moved to the big windows and looked through, hoping to spot him playing outside. Most boys didn't like to be cooped up indoors, and she figured Ian was no exception. Taking a chance, she opened the door and stepped outside, walking slowly around the perimeter of the Victorian, with no sign of Ian. With a sigh, she came back through the sunroom door and paused when her eyes lit on something on the chair.

It was Ian's phone.

She'd never seen him without his phone, most of the time glued to the gaming screen. The only time she'd seen him put the thing down was while they'd been watching movies the night before. The worry that had started with Miss Edna's phone call accelerated a gnawing feeling in the pit of her stomach. Something was wrong.

She turned at Miss Edna's approach. The older woman's

pallor worried her almost as much as Ian being missing. But she needed to ask the burning question now front and center in her brain.

"Miss Edna, Ian's phone is here. When's the last time you saw him?"

"About an hour before lunchtime. So, about one o'clock. He'd been sitting in here, playing his game. I'd put on a load of towels in the washer and headed upstairs. You don't think..." Her words trailed off and she raised a hand to her mouth.

"I'm sure he's fine. I'm going outside and see if he wandered too far into the woods. You stay here and call me if he comes back."

"I feel so guilty. Mr. Williamson called, and I assured him Ian was fine. I didn't bother to check on him, because I'd seen him a little while before. This is all my fault."

"It's nobody's fault, Miss Edna. I'll find him, I promise."

Miss Edna reached out and grasped Daisy's forearm. "Be careful."

"I will."

Without a backward glance, Daisy headed for the woods, praying she'd find Ian and bring him home again safe.

Ian shuffled along, although most of the way he stomped his feet, hoping the pounding act would scare away any more snakes. He'd picked up a branch, one that was about as big around as his wrist and as long as his arm, ready to use it as a weapon if he had to. The rain hadn't started yet, though a couple of times it had sprinkled. The trees blocked most of it, but he was scared. If it started raining, it might take forever before he found his way back to the B&B or somebody found him.

That's what he really wished for, somebody to realize he wasn't where he was supposed to be and come looking for him. Even if it meant he got into trouble, it'd be worth it, because at least he'd be safe from snakes. And cougars. And bears. He wasn't sure what else might be this deep into the woods, but he'd bet it would be dangerous.

A loud crack sounded followed by the sky brightening when lightning flashed overhead, accompanied by a loud clap of thunder. Dropping his stick, he slammed his hands against his ears, trying to block the noise. His heart began beating faster, and he felt like he was going to throw up.

"I want to go home," he whispered, trying not to start crying again. A scream broke from his throat when the bushes ahead rustled wildly, and he stumbled backward when something burst through, making a loud snuffling sound. It looked like a giant pig with horns growing out of its mouth. No, not horns. Tusks. It was dark brown or black, it was hard to tell without much light. Another rumble of thunder rolled, and the pig made a grunting sound, its enormous head swinging around, its eyes crazed. Until they landed on him.

Uh oh. He took a tentative step back, and the animal snorted, its beady eyes zeroed in on Ian. Panic racked him, and he frantically searched the ground for his stick, but it had rolled a few feet away. He was defenseless. If he ran, the pig would chase him. He couldn't outrun it, he knew. He wasn't athletic; heck, he barely passed his physical education classes.

What am I going to do? I don't want to die. Please, please, Dad, come and find me. I'll never run off again, I promise.

Another step back had the pig darting toward him, and Ian turned and ran, faster than he'd ever run. He darted between the tree trunks. With every step, he heard the creature gaining on him. Branches struck his shoulders and scraped his face as he raced past, adrenaline coursing through his body, giving him a burst of speed.

There! He knew he'd seen a tree that had boards fastened to it like steps. He hoped they held because it was his only chance. Sprinting for his life, he lunged for the first board, and wrapped his hand around it, pulling himself up and slammed his feet against the bottom one. He pulled himself up as fast as he could, using the slats of wood like a ladder, going hand over hand, desperation fueling his every move.

Below him on the ground, the hog stomped the ground and made the most excruciating sounds he'd ever heard. Another flash of lightning slashed across the sky, and he huddled against the trunk, sitting on an extended branch.

His arms were wrapped tightly around the tree, his lungs burning as he struggled to slow his breathing.

"Take that, you big pig! I beat you!"

The beast circled the base of the tree, and Ian found himself wondering if pigs could climb trees. He was in a heck of a lot of trouble if they could.

Without warning, the skies opened, and the rain let loose, coming so fast he could barely see a foot in front of his face. Wrapping his arms and legs around the tree as tight as he could, he kept watching the pig circle around beneath him, shaking its head, snot flying from his nose. The tusks protruding from it looked long and sharp.

The rain continued pelting him and within seconds, he was soaked to the skin. Closing his eyes, he wondered how he would ever get home. He was well and truly stuck up the tree with no way down. The pig had plopped onto the ground at the tree's base and didn't look like he was going anyway any time soon.

Unable to think of anything else he could do, Ian tried the one option he had left. He started praying.

CHAPTER SIXTEEN

Derrick climbed from Rafe's car, tired to his core. They'd found Jennifer Boatwright and her boyfriend exactly where Pamela Dobbins said they'd be, shacked up in a hotel room, waiting for her to get there with money for them to head to Oklahoma. Instead, they were currently ensconced at the Santa Lucia police station, waiting for Jennifer's aunt and uncle to arrive.

Rafe had turned the case over to the Santa Lucia police since they'd been found in their jurisdiction. Derrick didn't blame him. If given the choice, he'd have done the same. There'd still be tons of paperwork to go through, but at least the girl had been found safe and sound, even if she wasn't happy.

"Why is it I don't feel much like celebrating? We found the missing girl, everybody's going to end up going home healthy and happy at the end of the day, but I feel kind of deflated."

Derrick agreed with Rafe's sentiments. Sometimes he wondered if it was worth all the effort. He'd gone toe to toe with actual kidnappers, murderers, and the scum of the earth, and got a sense of satisfaction. Of a job well done. Cases like this one? Teenagers too young to realize they were making a huge mistake because they allowed their hormones and teen lust to overrule their common sense. There was young love—and then there was sheer stupidity.

"Maybe it's because there's no sense of catching the bad guy. Jennifer thought she was in love, and was being unfairly persecuted by her mother and the rest of the world. She still doesn't get it, that she disrupted the police, her family's friends and neighbors, and had an entire community looking for her. All she cared about were her own selfish desires, and her feelings overruling her brain."

"It burns me, how much time and money we've wasted. People searching for her, thinking she might be hurt or worse. Officers who should have been assisting the county's citizens, having to be pulled off helping folks who really needed it, to deal with a selfish, immature child."

"Speaking of children, I'd better call mine. He's avoided me all day."

"Like that, huh?"

"I'm a horrible father," Derrick echoed his son's words, and felt a surge of guilt, wondering if maybe there was a kernel of truth. "And honestly, if we hadn't been dealing with this missing girl case, I'd have probably found a way to work anyway, even if it was paperwork. I'm still trying to get the hang of having a nine-year-old."

"I'm sure you're doing better than you think. Everyone I

know says it's a balancing act, work and family."

Derrick gave a halfhearted laugh. "I'm just hoping there's a safety net."

Opening the door, they stepped inside. Sally Anne greeted Rafe with a hug, and she smiled at Derrick. "Sounds like y'all saved the day."

"Depends on who you ask." Rafe smiled at her and headed down the hall. Derrick pulled out his phone and decided to try and get in touch with Ian. Maybe he'd feel better if he knew he'd be home soon, and there'd be no more work for the rest of their stay. Tomorrow, the furniture should arrive, and they'd get to spend one night in their new house before heading back to Austin.

The phone rang and rang, eventually switching to voice mail, and Derrick disconnected without leaving a message. Hopefully, he'd only be here a few more minutes, and he'd be able to head back to the B&B.

After all the drama of dealing with the missing Boatwright girl, he'd be happy to spend some time with his son. Even if said son was royally ticked at him.

Daisy tracked through the woods, knowing the downpour would have washed away any footprints that might have been left. She hadn't wanted to admit it in front of Miss Edna, who already felt guilty enough, but she was worried. It wasn't like Ian to disappear. At least, Derrick had never mentioned his son doing something so irresponsible.

"Where are you, Ian?"

The rain poured down in torrents, and she was soaked to the bone, chill bumps rising on her skin. It had been warm this afternoon, but the temperature dropped when the storm rolled in, and being drenched made her even colder. There wasn't anything to make her believe Ian was in these woods, except her gut. Exploring them would have been almost irresistible for a boy Ian's age, especially one who'd grown up in the city.

Brushing aside the foliage, she traipsed deeper, calling out Ian's name every few minutes. She hoped against hope she'd find him, but wasn't going to count on it happening. The forested area behind the B&B was huge. Miss Edna owned a good chunk of the property, all the way to the creek to the north, and several acres to the east and west. The old Victorian was pretty much the southernmost point of the property, and Miss Edna, along with her family, hadn't wanted the land commercialized or developed. Instead, they preferred it to be left to its natural beauty.

"Ian, can you hear me?"

When no one answered, Daisy faltered, her shoe stuck in the clumpy mud. Rivulets of water snaked along the ground, making walking tricky. She wasn't ready to give up yet, though. Ian was here; she knew it. But it was getting darker, the sun blotted out by the ominous-looking clouds.

Derrick, where are you?

Knowing she should call Derrick, she reached into her pocket and patted it. She bit back a curse when she realized in her rush to get inside to Miss Edna, she'd tossed her phone onto the front seat of the car when she'd parked.

"Great, just great. Now I can't even call Derrick. He's going to have a conniption when he finds out his son's missing." Taking a deep breath, she yelled as loud as she could. "Ian? Can you hear me?"

"Help!"

She stopped in her tracks, hearing the voice cry out in response. It had to be Ian!

"Ian, call out again, as loud as you can!"

"Daisy, help me!"

It was hard to tell with the rain pouring down, but it sounded like his voice came from her right. Taking a deep breath, she turned and headed in that direction, skirting around fallen branches and small bushes blocking her path. The sharp crackle of lightning lit the sky, followed by an enormous boom of thunder, almost directly overhead. The rain intensified, dumping bucketsful onto the already saturated earth.

"Ian, I'm coming. Stay where you are." She shouted the words louder, praying he could hear her above Mother Nature's thunderstorm display. What a time for Texas weather to turn cranky. Couldn't it have waited until she found Ian?

"Daisy! Where are you?"

Ian's voice sounded closer, a little louder, and if she wasn't mistaken, coming from straight ahead. She stumbled over a buried root, and barely kept herself upright, grabbing onto the side of a tree. Rubbing her palm against the leg of her jeans, she walked forward, following the sounds.

"Keep talking, Ian. Are you okay?" It was hard keeping her voice raised with every word, but she'd do whatever it took to find Ian. The underlying panic in his voice let her know he was scared. Not that she blamed him; she would be too, if she took the time to think about the fact she was in the middle of a thunderstorm, surrounded by animals. She knew there were snakes and deer, and she'd heard there were a few feral hogs in the area. Which wouldn't be the best thing to run into, especially under these conditions.

"Daisy! Be careful. There's a monster under my tree!"

Under his tree. Guess that means he had to climb. But monster? Uh oh.

"What kind of monster?"

"A giant pig thing. It has sharp tusks in its mouth."

"I'm coming. Keep talking to me, Ian. You said you're up in a tree?"

"Yeah, I had to run to get away from this pig thing."

Daisy knew he meant a feral hog and felt a wave of thankfulness he'd gotten away from it. Feral hogs were fast, and they could be vicious when confronted. Ian didn't know how lucky he'd been.

"It's called a feral hog. Do you like ham? Because feral pigs taste like ham."

"Yuck. I don't want to eat him. I just want him to go away." His voice was getting louder. She hadn't even had to yell for him to hear her, so he had to be close. The rain had started lessening, though it was still dark as dusk.

Looking around, she picked up a dead branch lying on the ground. A couple of feet and she found another. Now all she had to figure out was how to get a feral hog to lose interest in a lone boy up a tree. No biggie.

"Is it still there?"

"Yes. I think it hears you because it stood up. What are we going to do?"

"You're not going to do anything except stay up in the tree. When I chase it away, be ready to climb down as fast as you can."

"Um, Daisy? I can't climb down. I don't know how to climb a tree."

Daisy stopped dead still, and closed her eyes, counting to ten. The whole situation just needed that little tidbit, didn't it?

"Don't worry, big guy, we'll figure it out once the hog's gone, 'kay?"

Tightening her grip on the two branches, she moved forward, listening intently. It wasn't long, probably less than a minute, before she heard snuffling sounds coming from almost straight in front of her. Great, she was close.

"Daisy?" Fear tinged Ian's voice, and she had to answer.

"I'm still here, buddy. Look to your left. I'm in front of you." She watched him searching frantically for her, watched his little body slump in relief when he spotted her.

"I see you."

"Great. Keep really still and quiet. I'll get you down. I promise."

She watched him wrap his arms tighter around the tree and nod.

Now all she had to do was scare off a feral hog, coax a terrified boy out of a tree, and get him back to the bed and breakfast in one piece.

Piece of cake.

CHAPTER SEVENTEEN

Seeing Miss Edna's name on the caller ID, Derrick answered after the first ring.

"Williamson."

"It's Edna from the Creekside Inn."

Immediately, he could tell she was stressed, and it sounded like she'd been crying.

"What's wrong? Is Ian okay?" Adrenaline shot through him, his heartbeat skyrocketing as worst-case scenarios raced through his mind.

"I'm so sorry. He's missing." Her words rushed together in panic, the deep gravely sound of her voice almost indistinguishable, blocked by tears.

"Missing. How long has he been gone?" Grabbing his hat off the table, he started for the door, but before he'd taken more than two steps, Antonio blocked his path. When he tried to move around him, he shifted, refusing to let him pass.

"I don't know. It's all my fault. I made lunch and left it for him on the table. I wasn't paying enough attention. If anything's happened to him, I'll never forgive myself."

"I'm on my way. Don't do anything until I get there. Call me back if he shows up." Disconnecting the call, he stared at Antonio. "Move."

"Not until you tell me what's wrong."

"Ian's missing, and you're keeping me from finding him. Now get out of my way."

"I'm going with you."

Derrick gave him a long stare, followed by a stiff nod. "Let's go."

Within minutes, Derrick pulled up in front of the B&B and raced up the front step, Antonio on his heels. Miss Edna sat in the lobby, her eyes red-rimmed. She looked up when they entered and immediately burst into tears again.

"Mr. Williamson, I can't tell you how sorry I am. Nothing like this has ever happened here before."

Antonio pushed past Derrick and knelt down in front of Miss Edna, gently clasping her hand between his. He was showing a lot more patience than Derrick felt, because inside he alternated between terrified and hot burning rage.

"Tell me what happened. When did you first notice Ian missing?"

"I made lunch for him. The last guest left earlier this morning, and I'd stripped the beds and gathered the towels. After I laid out the food, I went and put on a load of laundry, and did chores. When I came back downstairs, I noticed the plate still on the table untouched. I looked for Ian, but I couldn't find him anywhere."

"Where did you look for him?" Antonio kept his voice low, soft. Derrick had seen him in the field before, but it always surprised him how the agent seemed to know exactly what approach to take to get people to open up to him. It didn't hurt that Antonio knew the inn's owner personally.

"Everywhere. I even climbed the stairs to the attic and checked up there. Daisy even went outside and looked around and couldn't find him."

Derrick had been so caught up in getting to his son, he hadn't even noticed Daisy's car parked out front.

"Where's Daisy?"

Miss Edna's voice quivered, "She went into the woods looking for him."

Fear shot straight to Derrick's heart at the thought of his son alone in the woods. Ian hadn't spent much time in the great outdoors, having been born and bred in the city. His ex hated nature, and everything to do with dirt and bugs. He'd scoffed at her nonsense but let her have her way with keeping him isolated in the city. Was he going to pay for his pettiness now at his son's expense?

"That's good, Miss Edna." Antonio glanced at Derrick, motioning with his head toward the opening to the kitchen. Derrick gave him a brief nod and walked into the other room. Antonio asked the older woman a few more questions before joining him.

"Would Ian go into the words alone?"

"I don't know. If you'd asked me that twenty-four hours

ago, I'd have said no. He knows better, and I gave him specific instructions to stay inside the B&B. But he's unhappy with me, so who knows what he'd do."

"Miss Edna said she called Daisy around four, and she came right over. That means she's been out there looking for him a little over an hour. It might be taking her a while because of the rain."

Derrick started for the door in the sunroom, the one that led outside. "I'm going to look for them."

"Wait." Antonio followed him as far as the door, holding it open for Derrick. "I'm going to call the family, get them here as quickly as possible. We'll find him."

Something inside Derrick uncoiled at the other man's words. Knowing he had friends who had his back, no matter what. The Boudreaus had become his surrogate family without him even realizing it, making him an unofficial part of their clan.

"Thank you."

"I'll be right behind you. Go. Find your son."

Derrick took off across the backyard of the B&B, heading straight into the woods. The rain has lessened, but it hadn't stopped. The ground beneath his feet acted like quicksand, his feet disappearing into the sticky muck. Water sloshed against his legs, yet he pushed on. Ian was out here somewhere, and he had to find him.

Daisy was out here, too. She hadn't hesitated, hadn't pushed the responsibility for finding Ian onto someone else.

Instead, she'd pushed everything aside to look for his son. And he loved her for it. No, he realized, he was qualifying his feelings, making it sound like he only loved her because she sacrificed to find Ian. He loved her.

"Ian!" He called out, listening intently, hoping to hear something. "Daisy, can you hear me?"

Silence greeted him. Inside the forested area, the depth of darkness shrouding the area surprised him. The overcast sky from the earlier thunderstorm kept everything dark and gloomy, and he prayed Ian wasn't scared.

He jogged through the underbrush, though it was slow going, and he doubted he was the most graceful runner, but it got the job done. Moving forward, he looked for anything, any sign of clue which direction his son might have gone. If he was lucky, Daisy had found him, and they were on their way back.

A loud squeal rent the air coming from his right, the sound chilling him to the bone. It was an animalistic cry, high pitched and filled with pain.

Heart in his throat, he raced toward the sound, praying it hadn't come from his son.

Daisy eased forward, keeping the feral hog in her sight. The thing looked huge, though she supposed if she wasn't hyped up on adrenaline, it wasn't much bigger than a large dog. On the plus side, she figured it wasn't a momma, because she hadn't spotted hide nor hair of babies.

Balancing on the balls of her feet, she hefted one of the branches into the bushes, making as much noise as possible. The hog spun toward the noise, grunting and taking a few steps forward. Unfortunately, it didn't leave, instead freezing in place, its whole body quivering.

Breathing out slowly, she tossed the other branch like a javelin, arcing it through the air, and it flew into the same patch of bushes she'd hit before, shaking the leaves enough the hog darted toward it, barreling through them and making enough noise it hopefully scared away anything else that might have been hiding in the area.

"Daisy, is it gone?"

"Hang on a second, Ian. We need to make sure."

She looked around the forest floor, and while she didn't see any more branches large enough to use as a weapon, she did spot a fairly good size rock. Picking it up, she hefted it in her hand and smiled. Hopefully, she wouldn't have to use it, but you never know.

Moving cautiously, she finally stood directly beneath the tree where Ian was and looked up. Ian clung to the branches like a monkey, his arms and legs wrapped around it.

"Ian, I want you to loosen your grip on the tree, and—"

"Daisy, look out!"

She spun at his yell and found herself face to snout with the feral hog. It shook its head, knocking loose the dead branch attached to one tusk. When it spotted her, it snorted out an ugly sound that sent chills down her spine. Unless she could shimmy up the tree where Ian clung, there wasn't a chance she'd be able to outrun the beast.

There was only one thing she could do, the only option she had left. Pulling back her right arm, she channeled her inner softball pitcher and let the rock rip. It landed with a loud thunk—right between the hog's eyes.

The most horrendous sound came from the beast she'd ever heard. On the plus side, it spun and raced away, leaving muddy tracks in its wake. Slumping against the tree trunk, she let out a shaky laugh.

"Daisy, you did it!"

"Sure did. You ready to come down."

"Yes."

"Ian! Daisy! Where are you? Are you okay?"

"Dad!" Ian yelled. "We're over here."

Within a couple of minutes, Derrick burst through the underbrush and trees, skidding to a halt when he spotted her. She knew she had a goofy grin on her face, but it didn't matter. She'd never been so happy to see anybody in her whole life.

"Daisy, sweetheart, are you okay?"

"I am now." She flung herself into his arms and felt his arms wrap around her, her body trembling. Ian was safe, and they could all head back to the B&B. Wait, Ian! He was still up in the tree.

"Can somebody get me? I'm stuck."

Derrick glanced up and grinned, spotting his son several feet up. He winked at Daisy.

"You can do it. I'll be here to catch you if you fall."

And that was one of the reasons why she loved him. He was solid and steady, dependable, and he'd always be there for those he cared about. It was a heady thought because she was part of that inner circle. She knew they had a long way to go, and secrets to reveal before she could open fully to him and admit her feelings.

All she could hope was once he knew the truth, she wouldn't find herself out in the cold. Again.

CHAPTER EIGHTEEN

B y the time they'd made their way back to the B&B, the entire place was packed to the rafters with Boudreaus. Antonio, Rafe, and Heath had been on their way out the back door, ready to head into the woods. Douglas and Ms. Patti manned a command station in the kitchen, complete with walkie-talkies and Google Earth photos of the entire wooded area. Camille, Tessa, Serena, Miss Edna, and Beth were already gathering supplies: blankets, towels, and first aid kits were stacked and ready.

Derrick kept his arm around Daisy, keeping her pulled close to his side. He didn't miss the smirks coming from his friends, but being the bigger man, chose to ignore them. For now. Ian raced ahead, allowing himself to be wrapped in a hug from Ms. Patti.

"Good to see everybody's okay." Rafe studied their almost drowned appearance, and Derrick's arm tightened around Daisy. The rain had tapered off on their way back, and the sun peeked out from behind the clouds which rapidly headed east.

"It was touch and go for a bit." Daisy greeted him with a

smile. "I found Ian up a tree, pinned there by a feral hog."

"Whoa. He looks okay."

"That's because Daisy chased it off with a rock." Derrick didn't try to hide the pride he felt for her. She'd singlehandedly saved his son from what could have been a bad injury. As far as he was concerned, she was a bona fide hero.

Serena walked toward them and wrapped a blanket around Daisy's shoulders. Derrick reluctantly released her, and she went with Serena into the B&B.

"Dude, you've got it bad." Antonio clapped him on the shoulder. "Welcome to the club."

"What?"

"Seriously, are you going to try and tell us you're not head over heels for her?"

His eyes followed Daisy, watching her interact with the women, who handed her a hot drink, laughing and joking. Even covered with mud and twigs, she was the most beautiful thing he'd ever seen, and he didn't care who knew how he felt.

"I'm so far gone, there's no coming back. I just pray she feels the same."

"Derrick, you'd have to be blind not to see the woman loves you too." Rafe grinned and clapped him on the back. "Before you know it, you'll be living in Shiloh Springs permanently."

"We'll see."

"Seriously, dude, do you want me to call EMS to check

out Ian and Daisy?"

Douglas walked over, and hearing Antonio's question, he added, "I've already call Doc Stevens. I explained the situation, and he's waiting for us at the clinic."

Derrick grimaced, because he knew he had a fight on his hands. Ian *did not* like doctors. When he'd sprained his ankle a few months back, the resulting battle to get him examined had been a tug of war. One that Derrick won.

"I'll let them know we're on our way." Antonio and Rafe walked back toward the B&B, leaving him alone with Douglas. He admired the man. He'd guided a family of rebellious, troubled young boys into men any father would be proud of. Men he was proud to call his friends.

"Glad everything worked out. Ian's young and he'll bounce back from this. He'll look at it as an adventure when he's a bit older. A little time and distance will morph the terror into something less scary. But you'll remember the truth. My advice: don't blow it out of proportion or make it bigger than it was."

"I'm going to have nightmares for months. Knowing Ian was cornered by a feral hog? My heart may never recover."

Douglas' mouth curved into a smile. "It will. You have no idea how many adventures like this my boys got into over the years. I'm surprised I wasn't stone gray by the time I was forty."

"Thank goodness I only have one. I don't know how you did it with eleven."

"Don't forget Nica. That girl gave me more heart palpitations than all the boys put together. To look at her now, you'd never know she was a regular tomboy. And a troublemaker."

Derrick couldn't picture the lone Boudreau daughter as anything like what Douglas described, but he knew looks could be deceiving. He looked over at Daisy, with the Boudreau women fussing over her. Knew he couldn't— wouldn't—give her up. Not without a fight.

"You're perfect for her. Daisy's had a rough life. She needs somebody willing to accept her for who she is. Somebody who can settle and give her roots. A sense of permanence that she's craved for a long time. It won't be easy, because she carries a world of guilt on her shoulders and doesn't feel like she's worthy of forgiveness." Douglas stared at him, his expression closed off. "If you aren't willing to commit to her, love her unconditionally, I'm asking you to walk away now before her heart gets broken."

"If anybody but you spoke to me like that, I'd tell them to mind their own business. What's between me and Daisy is exactly that, between us. But I know you love her and want her to be happy. I love her. Ian loves her. I'm not saying it's going to be easy, but Antonio and Heath make it work commuting. I can, too."

At his statement, because there was no question in his heart Derrick meant every word he said, Douglas nodded and headed back into the B&B, apparently satisfied he wasn't planning on hurting Daisy. If there was one thing the Boudreaus were, it was fiercely loyal to the people they cared about, and Daisy was part of that inner circle. Maybe one day...

"Dad," Ian came running up to him. "Antonio says I have to go see the doctor. I don't want to. I'm not hurt."

"You might not feel like you're hurt, kiddo, but you were stuck in the pouring rain for a long time. We want to make sure you don't get sick. Besides," he leaned in and whispered in Ian's ear, "we're going to make Daisy go see the doctor too."

"Really?"

"Cross my heart. Think she's going to cause a stink?"

Ian giggled, and it sounded like music to Derrick. He loved his son so much, he couldn't bear to think of what might have happened if Daisy hadn't found him.

"Naw, Daisy ain't afraid of anything."

"Not true, Ian. I'm scared of lots of things." She walked across the yard and ruffled his hair. "The trick is to face them head-on. Tell them *I'm not afraid of you*. Most things don't seem so scary if you stand up to them or share your fears with somebody else."

Ian took a deep breath, then told her. "I'm scared of doctors."

Daisy knelt beside him and placed her hands on his shoulders. "I'm scared of doctors too. But I know Doc Stevens and Doc Jennings. I've talked to them, and I know they will never hurt me. Doc Jennings once told me it hurts him when he sees people in pain because his job is to make them feel better. No doctor will ever deliberately hurt you, not on purpose."

"Really?"

"Pinky swear." She held out her hand, extending her little finger, and Ian hooked his around hers. Derrick struggled to breathe at the sweetness overload. Ian seemed to take every word Daisy spoke as a pledge, a solemn promise. Didn't seem to matter that he'd basically told Ian the same thing. Guess coming from a woman gave it a different meaning.

"Ready to go?"

"Yes, sir." Ian gave him a jaunty salute, his crooked grin something Derrick cherished, because for the longest time his son hadn't smiled. Not nearly enough.

"Yes, sir," Daisy mimicked, complete with the salute. Ian grabbed her hand and began tugging her toward the B&B's door, leaving Derrick to trail behind.

A few hours later, everyone had returned home. Ian was tucked into bed, having endured the doctor visit better than Derrick could have hoped, and been given a clean bill of health. Doc Stevens warned him to keep a close eye on him for the next couple of days, and if he started coughing or seemed to be coming down with a cold, to bring him back, or take him to see his physician in Austin.

He'd called his boss, and explained he'd need a few extra

days off. It wasn't a problem, since he had a ton of vacation and sick time accrued. Before Ian had moved in with him, he never took time off. Working long hours was easier than dealing with the loneliness of a condo without anybody to come home to.

Going to bed didn't hold any appeal, so he pulled the covers up on Ian's chest, and quietly left the room. He'd go downstairs, maybe grab a cup of coffee.

When his text alert signaled, he pulled out his phone and noticed it was from Daisy. She asked if she could come over and talk. He immediately texted back and she responded, saying she'd be there in a couple of minutes.

His gut clenched. He knew this was *the conversation*. The one he'd known was coming almost from the moment they'd met. Without a doubt, she was coming to tell him they were over. To sever things before they got too complicated to step back from. She'd already decided to cut and run because she wasn't ready to face her feelings for him.

Too bad. He had no intention of letting her get away. Not now. Not ever.

CHAPTER NINETEEN

Daisy smoothed her hands down her jean-clad legs, wondering for the hundredth time if she was ready for this conversation. Inside she was a riot of emotions, ranging from worry to fear to resignation. Best to bite the bullet, endure the pain, and get out.

Taking a deep breath, she opened the front door to the B&B. It wasn't so late that Miss Edna would have locked up. Besides, Derrick was expecting her.

Derrick leaned against the opening to the kitchen, a coffee cup in his hand. Her hands began sweating, and she felt like she was about to throw up.

This is ridiculous. Get it over with, there's no need to draw things out. Spit it out and let the truth come into the light. He'll dump you the minute he finds out anyway. Why prolong the inevitable?

"How's Ian?"

"Sound asleep. Kids are resilient. He dropped off the minute his head hit the pillow."

"That's good. I doubt I'll sleep a wink. It's been playing over and over in my head. What if I'd been a few minutes later finding him? What if he fell?"

Derrick walked toward her and handed her the cup, and she looked inside, finding it contained hot chocolate with tiny marshmallows. The warmth from the cup heated her cold hands. After they'd been checked out at the clinic, she'd headed home and taken the longest shower in history. The whole while she'd stewed, wondering if she dared tell Derrick the truth about her past. It was agony, sheer torture, vacillating between keeping it to herself and always having a sword of Damocles hanging over her head, or risking everything for a chance at happiness.

"Ian's a strong kid. He might be little, but he's mature beyond his years. We had a long talk while the doctor was checking him out, and he understands the consequences of his actions. A heaping helping of guilt over his foolish actions, doing exactly what he knew he'd been forbidden to do, and being grounded for the rest of his life seemed a small price to pay for him being safe. Have I told you how grateful I am that you found him? I don't think I'll ever get over seeing you standing at the base of that tree. Did I tell you I heard the squeal from the hog? I thought it was you or Ian, and I—"

She touched his hand gently. "Nobody got hurt. We're home, safe and sound. Tomorrow, you'll move into your new house and start over."

"I need a drink. Come on."

He turned and walked into the kitchen and poured a cup

of coffee. Carrying it to the sunroom, he sat on the loveseat and patted the seat beside him. Swallowing, she followed and took the seat, then had second thoughts. Maybe she should have sat in the chair instead, putting some distance between them. Being this close, telling him what she'd done, was going to be one of the hardest things she'd ever had to do.

"I need to talk to you."

"I'm right here. You can tell me anything." Derrick took a sip of coffee, a tiny quirk of his lip making her want to reach out and touch it. Touch him, maybe for the last time. This was stupid, having these kinds of feelings for a man she hadn't even kissed. How crazy was that?

"There's something you should know. About me. About my past."

"You can tell me anything, Daisy. I won't judge you."

"Don't make promises you can't keep." She wrapped both hands around her cup, letting the warmth seep into her. "Before I came to Shiloh Springs, I got into some trouble. Legal trouble."

"Alright. Tell me everything."

"Usual story. I was young and stupid. Thought I was in love. His name was James. A typical bad boy, but then I was a rebel. Did the opposite of everything I should. If it was fast, fun, or questionable, you could count me in. I got arrested when I was eighteen for drugs. They let me go because it was a first-time offense."

He leaned back and put his feet up on the coffee table in

front of them, crossing them at the ankles. "Sounds like it wasn't the last time. Keep going."

Narrowing her eyes, she studied his relaxed posture, wondering what was going through that big brain. Surely he could see where this was headed. He wouldn't want a convicted felon around his son.

"I stayed with James for three years. My mom didn't care what I did, as long as she got what she wanted, which was money and booze. I didn't deny her anything, because I liked living on the edge. The cheap thrills, the excitement of skating around the truth. Because my truth was ugly. I trusted James, did everything he asked. Not that it makes a difference, but I never did the hard stuff. Strictly weed and an occasional pill. I hated myself, and it was easier to stay high than to face the fact I was a lousy human being, headed toward a life in and out of jail."

"Seems like you turned yourself around. You are a business owner. You have friends who care about you. A community you serve. You're kind. I'm not seeing the issue."

She shook her head, unable to believe he was being this obtuse. Couldn't he read between the lines, realize they'd never work?

"Derrick, I didn't turn myself around. Well, I did, but not the way you think. I stayed with James despite knowing he was getting in deeper and deeper with more than just penny-ante stuff. He and his brother started robbing gas stations and convenience stores. Got in deep with local loan sharks. I probably know more about the ugly side of life than any other woman you know."

Or dated.

"I don't know about that. In my line of work, I've met some pretty sketchy women."

"Will you listen?" Was he deliberately being hardheaded? She bit back the urge to scream. Didn't he understand what she was telling him? No one in Shiloh Springs knew about her past. It was shameful and filled her with remorse. It didn't matter that she'd paid her debt to the people who'd been hurt. Even now, the thought mortified her, that she'd been naïve and gullible, all because of a man.

No, it's not right to put all the blame on James. You chose to be with him. He never forced you to do drugs. You liked the thrill, the riding high on the edge.

She rubbed her wrist, remembering the feel of handcuffs being snapped shut. Sitting in front of the judge, with the public defender beside her. Accepting the plea deal being offered by the district attorney. The bright orange jumpsuit. The numbness she'd felt for months, realizing she'd thrown her life away. Those years she'd never get back.

Derrick raised a hand. "I'm still listening. Not judging, just listening." He made a motion for her to continue.

"I can't do this. I thought I could, but I can't." Putting her cup on the table, she jumped to her feet. "I love you, Derrick. I have from the beginning, even when you barely noticed me. But we can't be together. I can't be around Ian.

I'm a convicted felon. I spent two years in prison. I drove the car when James and his brother robbed a fast-food place. I never went inside, didn't even know they were going to steal anything." She gave an ugly laugh. "I was so stupid. They said they were going to get us something to eat. Then they came running out and jumped in, screaming for me to drive. I panicked and hit the accelerator. Slammed right into the back end of a police car."

"I know."

"What?"

He stood, took her hands in his and leaned forward, looking her straight in the eye, his gaze never wavering. "I know everything. All of it. Do you honestly think I let anybody get close to my son without knowing every detail about their life and their history? Daisy, I work for the FBI. It took me all of ten minutes to know everything about you."

Pulling on her hands, she tried to break free, but Derrick refused to release her. She tugged harder but couldn't get him to turn her loose.

"Let go."

"Never. The only thing you've said tonight that matters is that you love me. Anything else we'll get past. Do you think you're the only person who's ever been in trouble? Who's ever made mistakes? While I've didn't get arrested, I haven't exactly been the poster boy for good works, Daisy."

"Derrick, you don't understand. No one in Shiloh Springs knows about me. About what I did. It would destroy me if they found out. I've made a place for myself here. I know you won't understand, but this town, these people, they are the only thing in my life that's kept me on track. They've accepted me, given me the kind of life I never dreamed was possible. It would break something inside me that would never heal if they hated me."

Derrick pulled her against his chest, and she struggled but couldn't break his hold. With a sigh, she allowed her head to fall against his chest. His amazing, rock-hard chest.

"Daisy, I want you to think for a second. What family basically runs this town?"

Her answer was immediate. "The Boudreaus."

"Exactly. And what do the Boudreaus specialize in?"

"Um…law enforcement and…" Her words trailed off as she realized his implication.

"Security." His answer softly echoed in her brain.

"They know." It wasn't a question.

"I'd be shocked if they didn't. They accept you for who you are, not for what you did in your misspent youth. Besides, think about all those Boudreau men. Every single one of them comes with a past they'd just as soon forget. Somehow, I doubt any of them blame you. Unless you've broken some law since you've lived in Shiloh Springs."

"No." Lightness began to fill her, a glowing warmth of acceptance. Derrick was right; the Boudreaus had probably known about her past all along. And they hadn't judged or condemned her. Just the opposite.

"Now, let's talk about you're loving me. Did you mean it?"

"Yes." She felt a rush of heat flood her face. What was the point of denying it?

"That's good, because I love you too. Daisy, sweet Daisy, you are my whole world. When Ian came into my life, I knew I had to focus on him, give him my whole attention. His life had been upended, and I couldn't afford for him to feel unwanted. But this whole time, I couldn't get you out of my mind, out of my thoughts. No matter how many times I tried not to see you, I kept coming back. Whenever I came to Shiloh Springs, it was always about work. Until I met you. I couldn't stay away. I love you, Daisy Parker."

She smiled at him. "Do you realize you've never kissed me?

"I'm aware."

Running a finger down his chest, she asked, "Don't you think you should remedy that?"

"I thought you'd never ask."

Swooping in, his lips landed against hers. There was nothing gentle or timid about his kiss. It evoked. It demanded. It devoured. She kissed him back with everything she had, pouring her love into their embrace. The moment seemed caught in time, and she wished she could stay in his arms forever.

"Dad?"

Derrick pulled back, and Daisy ran a hand over her hair,

embarrassed at being caught. Though she wasn't embarrassed or ashamed of what she felt in Derrick's arms. Nothing had felt so right in a long time.

"Ian, what's wrong?"

"I woke you and couldn't find you." His voice quivered, and Daisy walked over and put her arm around his shoulder, squeezing him gently.

"I couldn't sleep. Daisy and I were…talking."

Ian snickered. "You didn't look like you were talking."

"Ian!" Daisy felt the blush spreading across her face again.

"What? I'm just telling what I saw."

"Does it bother you? That I was kissing Daisy?"

Ian shook his head. "Nope. You know what this means, right?"

Derrick looked at Daisy, and she shrugged, having no idea what Ian was thinking.

"What does it mean?"

"Now you've got to marry her. That's what happens in all those sappy romance movies."

Daisy watched Derrick's shoulders move with suppressed laughter.

"Well, Daisy, you heard the man. Now you've got to marry me."

Was he serious? You didn't get married because your kid wants you to. That was insane. Wasn't it?

Derrick leaned in close to Ian, and whispered, "I don't

think she believes me. Maybe you'd better ask her if she'd marry us."

Ian's eyes lit with excitement. "Daisy, will you marry us? Me and my dad? I think it's a great idea."

Derrick winked at her. "I think it's a great idea, too."

Throwing caution to the wind, Daisy did the only thing that made sense.

She said yes.

CHAPTER TWENTY
EPILOGUE

Two Months Later

D ane raised his glass of lemonade as another toast to the happy couple was made. Seeing Daisy so happy thrilled him. She'd been a good friend for many years, and knowing she'd found somebody to love, who accepted her for who she was and didn't try to change her, gave him a great deal of satisfaction. More than once they'd shared coffee late at night and commiserated about their lives. She'd been there when he'd needed a confidant, somebody he could confide in, who wasn't a relative. While he adored his family, sometimes talking to somebody who didn't share that familial bond was not only beneficial, it saved his sanity.

Now she had Derrick Williamson and his son, Ian, to fulfill her, give her a renewed joy and purpose in life. Good for her—and Derrick—as long as he made her happy. If he didn't, well, he'd find Dane on his doorstep one night, and he wouldn't be there for tea and crumpets.

"Hey, bro. Why so down in the dumps?" Liam bumped his shoulder against his.

Dane shrugged. He couldn't explain exactly why he wasn't feeling himself lately. Maybe there was something in the air. Whatever it was, it managed to keep him on edge, and more than a little irritable. He'd snapped at one of the ranch hands this morning, all because the guy hadn't moved as fast as Dane wanted. He'd apologized and smoothed things, but it hadn't changed the sense of something hovering just over the horizon. Something that would change his life. Too bad he had no clue what it might be.

"Nothing in particular. What do you think of Williamson moving full-time to Shiloh Springs? I thought he and Ian were only going to be hanging around on weekends and stuff."

"I think Momma might have had something to do with that. She mentioned she might have put a bug in Antonio's ear to have a chat with Derrick about the commute. I think she's anxious to see him and Daisy take their relationship to the next level. People in the city do commutes just as long or longer to their jobs. He'll still be able to keep his job with the FBI in Austin. Ian will be able to go to school here. Daisy will watch him in the afternoons until Derrick gets home. Beats trying to do a long-distance relationship."

"I guess." Dane pointed to Ian, who sat beside Ms. Patti, talking up a storm. In the few months since they'd settled down in Shiloh Springs, the kid had come out of his shell, realizing he finally had a stable and loving home, and his father wasn't going to leave him.

Ian had come out to the Big House several times with his dad. The kid was crazy about the horses and probably would have moved into the barn if he could've talked his dad into it. Maybe he should talk to Derrick about giving Ian riding lessons.

"Boys." Dane chuckled when Liam flinched. He'd seen his father walking toward them, but hadn't clued his brother to his approach. He grinned when Liam jumped. He'd have thought, working with his dad every day, he'd have a sixth sense when it came to his father's sneak attacks.

"Hi, Dad. Nice party."

Douglas looked over to where his wife sat, Ian so close beside her he practically sat in her lap, Derrick and Daisy standing close by. A contented smile flitted across his father's face, and Dane realized his dad enjoyed having another young boy to mentor and help through life.

"Your momma gets all the credit. You know how she loves having y'all together in one place. She's in her element, surrounded by all her kids."

"Ian sure has latched onto her."

"Ian's a good kid. He simply needs a woman's love. Now he's got Daisy and your momma, it won't be long before he blossoms under the attention. He's gonna be a fine man one day."

Liam and his father started talking, mostly about work, and Dane tuned them out because once they got started on construction and building, he lost interest. Though he occasionally went and helped on their job sites, especially when they were under a time crunch and needed all able bodies on deck, it wasn't something that interested him. He needed to be outdoors, breathing the fresh air, and working with the livestock. That's where he felt most at home.

He caught Daisy's gaze from across the room and smiled when she started making her way across the diner. She'd worked with his momma to have this family get together after the diner had closed because she considered the Boudreaus family. Just like they considered her one of their clan.

"Most of the night, you've looked like you're a million miles away. Anything wrong?"

"No, I'm just feeling restless. It'll pass."

She studied his face intently, looking for what he didn't know, and he deliberately kept it blank. No need to let her in on the fact that there was a quirky, tattooed brunette who'd been haunting his thoughts and starring in his steamy, X-rated dreams.

"I'm not buying it. Who is she?"

He started at her blunt question, shooting a look at his father and brother, hoping they hadn't heard her question.

"Daisy—"

"Don't you Daisy me. You didn't mind sticking your nose into my business when I started seeing Derrick, letting me know exactly what you thought of him and assuring me that I wasn't making the biggest mistake in my life. I trust you to look out for my best interests because we are friends. Heck, we're more than friends; you're the brother of my heart. Now tell me what's wrong. It must be a woman, because you wouldn't have any problem telling me if it was one of your family members, or something going on at the ranch. Do I know her?"

He blew out a deep breath and took a long drink of the now warm lemonade he held. She was right, he thought of her as a sister. Like Nica. At least she wasn't a pain in the backside like his little sister, because she'd be all up in his business if she thought for a single instant he was interested in someone. Dang, he missed the little monster. She hadn't been able to come down because of school. Over the last several months, she'd missed too much time, and although she had stellar grades, she planned to graduate soon and needed to focus on her studies to make sure her grade point average didn't suffer.

"Tonight's the time to focus on you and your new family, Daisy. I promise, my problems will wait until later."

She shot him a narrow-eyed glare. "So, you admit there is a problem." It wasn't a question.

"Wrong choice of words. It's not a problem, more a feeling. Nothing concrete to pin my lousy mood on."

"Are you sure? Because we can always go and talk—"

"Absolutely not," Dane insisted. "This is your night. Now, tell me you're happy, and make me believe it."

The smile on Daisy's face told the story, along with the

glow of happiness that seemed to surround her. Though she and Derrick were engaged, thanks to Ian, they were taking it slow, getting to know each other the way newly engaged couples did. But if Dane had to bet, he'd lay down money they'd make it for the long haul.

"We're happy, Dane. With all the stuff in my past, I never thought I'd find somebody who could look beyond all the legal stuff and see me. He loves me. I love him. We both know it's fast, but it's real. More real than anything ever in my life, and it's only getting better every day."

Dane pulled her into his arms and gave her a tight hug, and her arms wrapped around him, squeezing. He looked at the sound of a throat clearing beside him, and knew it was Derrick before he even glanced up. He placed a soft kiss against her forehead and loosened the hug.

"Go. Know I wish you both every happiness. All you must do is love each other with all your hearts, and everything else will take care of itself. That's what my momma always says, and I believe her."

"Thanks, Dane. Don't forget, we're still going to talk. Soon."

Giving Daisy a nod, he watched her walk away, Derrick's arm around her waist. His phone vibrated in his pocket. He'd made sure to turn off the ringer before the party started, and he pulled it out, noting he'd missed four calls from an unknown number. He debated for a second whether to answer it because he really didn't want to deal with some robo-caller trying to sell him an extended car warranty. But some little niggling feeling made him decided to see who the mystery caller might be.

Stepping outside, he dialed the number.

"Why haven't you answered your phone?"

He pulled it away from his ear and stared at it for a second. Somebody had their panties in a bunch. The voice sounded familiar, but he couldn't place it.

"I'm not sure who you're looking for, lady, but—"

"Dane Boudreau. It's Destiny. We need to talk."

"Destiny?" A vivid picture of the sexy hacker who worked for his brother popped into his head. It wasn't hard, since he hadn't been able to stop thinking about her, though he hadn't seen her in a couple of months. The last time, he'd been given a firsthand, up-close view of her tattoos, especially the one that usually played peekaboo under the edge of her shirt.

"Yeah. Listen, we need to talk. Can you meet me?" She sounded frazzled, her words spilling out in a rush. He frowned because she didn't seem the type to get befuddled or harassed. At least, that had been his impression of her, based on their meeting and what Ridge had said about his resident computer hacker.

"When?"

"Now. I'm here, I mean I'm in Shiloh Springs. Where are you?"

"At the diner. There's a family gathering, kind of a celebration. Why don't you come over and join us?"

"Nuh-uh. Not a good idea. I should probably talk to you without any of your family around."

Now his curiosity was piqued. Why would Destiny seek him out? Aside from the teasing when she and Tina had been in the Big House kitchen, he hadn't seen or heard from her since. Now she wanted to meet him alone? Oh, well, he was game.

"Do you know where Juanita's is?"

"Yes. Can you leave now and meet me ASAP?" There was an almost desperate sound to her words, and he had a lightbulb moment. This was it. The thing that had been hovering on the horizon, tantalizing deceptively out of sight, keeping him pondering his future.

"Yes."

"Okay, I'll meet you there under one condition?"

Destiny's sigh was loud over the line. "What?"

"Tell me what's so important you don't want my family to know?"

"I've been doing some digging on the dark web, looking for some info, and came across your name."

"My name? Why would my name show up on the dark web?"

There was a long pause, and he could almost hear her brain racing, trying to come up with a reason not to tell him.

"Dane, somebody's put a hit out on your life."

Thank you for reading Derrick, Book #9 in the Texas Boudreau Brotherhood series. I hope you enjoyed Derrick and Daisy's story. I loved writing their book. Even though Derrick isn't a Boudreau, he's an honorary member of the clan, and when the chips are down, the Boudreaus always circle the wagons to protect one of their own. Plus, Daisy deserved her chance at happily ever after, don't you think?

Since so many readers wrote me, asking about some of the secondary characters in Shiloh Springs, I decided some of them deserved to have their own stories told, and allow them to get their *happily ever after*. This doesn't mean you won't be getting the rest of the Texas Boudreau brothers, it simply means you're getting additional books about the folks living in Shiloh Springs and their interactions with the family.

Next up is Dane Boudreau. Dane handles all the day-to-day workings of the Boudreau spread, keeping the ranch up and running. But when feisty Destiny, computer hacker extraordinaire, contacts him about a not-so-veiled threat to his life, Dane knows all his secrets are about to be exposed. Want to know more? Keep reading for an excerpt from his book, Dane, Book #10 in the Texas Boudreau Brotherhood. Available at all major e-book and print book stores. Available for pre-order now.

DANE

(Book #10 Texas Boudreau Brotherhood series)
© Kathy Ivan

LINKS TO BUY DANE:

www.kathyivan.com/Dane.html

"You dropped your bombshell and hung up before I could ask any questions." Dane leaned back against the padded back of the booth and crossed his arms over his chest. "Care to give me a few more details?"

Destiny stared down at her hands, twining her fingers over and over. All that nervous energy needed to go someplace. It was almost like she wanted—no, needed—to be working a keyboard rather than sitting here. Unfortunately, this wasn't a social meeting, where he could simply let her off the hook and send her on her way. No, the information she'd uncovered might make the difference in his own investigation. One nobody, especially not his family, knew about.

This was personal.

"Like I said, I like Ridge. He's a decent boss and lets me do my job on my own terms. He's talked about your family and how much you all mean to him. So, I've kinda kept my eyes open whenever I see the Boudreau name pop up online. Thank goodness you don't spell your last name like the Louisiana Boudreauxs. Having that X on the end really skews the results."

"From what I understand, generations ago our family did spell it with the X on the end. I have no idea when it changed, but…"

Destiny blew out a breath, and it ruffled the bangs across her forehead in a cute way. Most of the time he loved long hair on women, something he'd never questioned. But Destiny's hair was short, feathered in layers around her face, and it highlighted her high cheekbones and made her deep brown eyes seem huge.

"I set up a few alerts so any time one of your names popped up, from somebody doing an inquiry to a credit check, I got notified. Ninety-nine percent of the time it's nothing. Almost everybody who's on the internet has tons of stuff moving through sites and they never know. Usually, they are surface inquiries. Like when somebody looks up Camilla, because of her books. Things like that I discard without a second look. Ms. Patti's real estate business, Douglas' construction company? Tons of hits, but nothing that would raise any red flags."

"But something about my name did?"

She nodded, her teeth nibbling on her lower lip. Dane fisted his hands to keep from reaching across the table and touching her lip, to pull it free. He wasn't sure why he was reacting to Destiny like this. But ever since he'd seen her in the Big House's kitchen with Tina, seeing the tattoo on her chest, he couldn't stop thinking about her. And that was a problem. Until he'd settled his own life, he couldn't even think about dealing with anything, or anybody, else.

"How much do you know about the internet?"

Dane barely refrained from rolling his eyes. While he wasn't a complete noob, he had more than a passing knowledge of the ins and outs. Not as much as Destiny, obviously, but still...

"I get by."

"There is the internet, the world wide web, where almost everyone does their daily business. Whenever you do any kind of search, that's where you're looking. But there is a deeper layer, called the Dark Web. That's where a lot of your more...questionable...searches and requests happen."

Dane nodded, following her meaning. "I've heard of the Dark Web. That's where you found my name?"

"Yeah. At first I thought it was a mistake. Sometimes that happens. Some idiot types in a wrong URL and gets steered to a place where they'd never really know, and usually gets redirected pretty quick."

Destiny stopped talking when the waitress brought their drinks, along with chips, salsa and queso. Dane tapped the corner of the menu, and she shook her head, choosing instead to grab a tortilla chip and scoop up a mound of queso and pop it into her mouth. His mouth curved upward at the look of total bliss on her face. Well, that answered one question. The woman liked Mexican food.

"Let's cut to the chase, Destiny. You got an alert with my name. Found somebody had put a hit on me. What else do you have? A time? A place? A name? Give me something."

Her perusal made him feel like a bug under a microscope. She didn't say a word, simply studied him with such intensity he wanted to do something. Anything. Mostly he wanted to bolt from the restaurant, pretend he'd never heard about somebody wanting him dead. Unfortunately, that wasn't an option. He'd managed to stay hidden from the rest of the world for most of his life. Living with the Boudreaus, being adopted at a young age, had helped keep his pursuers off his trail for almost two decades.

But, if they had his name, that meant they'd found him.

LINKS TO BUY DANE:
www.kathyivan.com/Dane.html

NEWSLETTER SIGN UP

Don't want to miss out on any new books, contests, and free stuff? Sign up to get my newsletter. I promise not to spam you, and only send out notifications/e-mails whenever there's a new release or contest/giveaway. Follow the link and join today!

http://eepurl.com/baqdRX

REVIEWS ARE IMPORTANT!

People are always asking how they can help spread the word about my books. One of the best ways to do that is by word of mouth. Tell your friends about the books and recommend them. Share them on Goodreads. If you find a book or series or author you love – talk about it. Everybody loves to find out about new books and new-to-them authors, especially if somebody they know has read the book and loved it.

The next best thing is to write a review. Writing a review for a book does not have to be long or detailed. It can be as simple as saying "I loved the book."

I hope you enjoyed reading Derrick, Texas Boudreau Brotherhood Book #9.

If you liked the story, I hope you'll consider leaving a review for the book at the vendor where you purchased it and at Goodreads. Reviews are the best way to spread the word to others looking for good books. It truly helps.

BOOKS BY KATHY IVAN

www.kathyivan.com/books.html

TEXAS BOUDREAU BROTHERHOOD
Rafe

Antonio

Brody

Ridge

Lucas

Heath

Shiloh

Chance

Derrick

Dane (coming soon)

NEW ORLEANS CONNECTION SERIES
Desperate Choices

Connor's Gamble

Relentless Pursuit

Ultimate Betrayal

Keeping Secrets

Sex, Lies and Apple Pies

Deadly Justice

Wicked Obsession

Hidden Agenda

Spies Like Us

Fatal Intentions

New Orleans Connection Series Box Set: Books 1-3
New Orleans Connection Series Box Set: Books 4-7

CAJUN CONNECTION SERIES
Saving Sarah
Saving Savannah
Saving Stephanie
Guarding Gabi

LOVIN' LAS VEGAS SERIES
It Happened In Vegas
Crazy Vegas Love
Marriage, Vegas Style
A Virgin In Vegas
Vegas, Baby!
Yours For The Holidays
Match Made In Vegas
One Night In Vegas
Last Chance In Vegas
Lovin' Las Vegas (box set books 1-3)

OTHER BOOKS BY KATHY IVAN
Second Chances (Destiny's Desire Book #1)

ABOUT THE AUTHOR

USA TODAY Bestselling author Kathy Ivan spent most of her life with her nose between the pages of a book. It didn't matter if the book was a paranormal romance, romantic suspense, action and adventure thrillers, sweet & spicy, or a sexy novella. Kathy turned her obsession with reading into the next logical step, writing.

Her books transport you to the sultry splendor of the French Quarter in New Orleans in her award-winning romantic suspense, or to Las Vegas in her contemporary romantic comedies. Kathy's new romantic suspense series features, Texas Boudreau Brotherhood, features alpha heroes in small town Texas. Gotta love those cowboys!

Kathy tells stories people can't get enough of; reuniting old loves, betrayal of trust, finding kidnapped children, psychics and sometimes even a ghost or two. But one thing they all have in common – love and a happily ever after). More about Kathy and her books can be found at

WEBSITE: www.kathyivan.com

Follow Kathy on Facebook at facebook.com/kathyivanauthor

Follow Kathy on Twitter at twitter.com/@kathyivan

Follow Kathy at BookBub
bookbub.com/profile/kathy-ivan

DISCARD

Made in the USA
Monee, IL
21 September 2021

78542203R00118